A Small Country
Siân James

Introduction by Stan Barstow

seren

seren
is the book imprint of
Poetry Wales Press Ltd
Wyndham Street, Bridgend, Wales

© Siân James, 1979, 1999
Introduction © Stan Barstow, 1999

First published in 1979
This edition published in 1999

ISBN 1-85411-258-9

A CIP record for this title is available from
the British Library

The publisher works with the financial assistance of the
Arts Council of Wales

Cover painting: 'View from the Hills' by James Mackeown

Printed in Plantin by
CPD Wales, Ebbw Vale

Introduction

We know we are in a real and fully apprehended world the moment we hear the railway porter's voice on page one of Siân James' absorbing novel. With what sureness she launches her tale. It is a model opening. If it has famously been said (though I can never remember by whom) that good dialogue should do three things – reveal character, convey information and move the story along – here it is in the hands of a writer of high skill. And if the years in which her story is set were before her own time she nevertheless manages to convey throughout the authenticity of a life known, felt and closely observed.

The railway porter is garrulous. Siân James is not. As my gaze drifts idly over the great slabs of fiction on airport bookshelves nowadays I am irresistibly reminded of the man who apologized to his correspondent when he said, winding up: "I'm sorry I've written you such a long letter, but I didn't have time to write a short one". Verbosity is not one of Siân James' characteristics, which is why she is also such a good short-story writer. There are many, many lesser talents who (most of them incapable of anything else) might have drawn out her story to twice the length of *A Small Country* and, regrettably, attracted many times the audience from that readership which is never happier than when plodding along to the sounds of every 't' being crossed, every 'i' dotted.

When Siân James brings you a scene full-face it pulses with life and physical passion; but often she will let another scene occur off-stage and merely report it in summary. So with her characters. Some we comprehend more thoroughly than others. We believe the rage of love which brings together the errant Josi Evans and his tragic mistress, Miriam; but do we know them through and through? Mrs James is not in the business of psychoanalysis, and their predicament is the more poignant for what is left unsaid, "The heart has its reasons..." The sense of life going on at the edges of her story, and outside it, lends what she tells an unstrained conviction.

We are in deepest rural Wales just before the First World War and among people of substance and standing. Rachel Griffiths rejected the man her father approved of her marrying for the son of one of his tenant farmers. Not that Josi Evans ever sought material advantage; and whatever drew him to Rachel has for some time now not been enough. A child born to his schoolteacher mistress resolves him to break free of his marriage. His grown children by Rachel look on with a bitterness that turns to pity and compassion as the tragedy of this relationship is played out.

The war, when it comes, seems so distant. Everyone talks as if it will be over in a few months. But gradually its tentacles reach out to draw them in. Tom, the son, just home from Oxford and with a farm to run now that his father has left, nevertheless feels impelled to volunteer; Catrin, his young sister, disappointed in her love for Tom's English friend Edward (who has already joined up), leaves home for the demanding life of a nurse. Ironically, at the novel's end with Rachel dead also, it is Josi who comes closest to real peace; Josi tuned to the pulse of life in a way that others can only envy, among them his son, Tom, who observes him after his defection: "There was little ceremony about his father; no fuss, no show. He suddenly saw him resting at the side of a hedge, his whole body completely relaxed so that he seemed almost a part of the landscape. He seemed extraordinarily at peace with himself; even at the present time, with his life completely disrupted...". Siân James creates moments of great tenderness between Josi and the young servant girl, Lowri, whom he asks to share his future, and shows a gift for corrective comedy in the reaction of the aged Grandfather after the wedding:

'Are you going to the war?' the old man asked.
'Too old, man,' Josi said.
'Too old?' The old man cleared his throat noisily.
'You think I should fight do you?' Josi asked amiably.
'For the bloody English. No.' The little man spat squarely into the flames.
'They wanted me to fight once; against the Russians, I think, or the Turks. Not I. My family fight against the bloody English, not for them...'
'Lloyd-George is a good little man to my way of thinking,' Josi said peaceably, 'and he's one of the English now.'
'Turn-coat from the North.'
'Good little man to my way of thinking,' Josi said again. 'Not my business, though. Not today.'

The old man spun round to face him, the light of understanding in his eyes at last.

'You're the bridegroom, are you?'

'Aye,' Josi said. 'That's right.'

'You old ram.'

It is, perhaps, in Edward's letter to Catrin, written from the trenches, that the heart of *A Small Country* is expressed: "Life can't be so frail that it can be quenched by a stray bullet or a piece of shrapnel. Surely it can't. There must be something more. It has taken a war to make me recognize the eternal in life, the river that flows through us all, so that there is no real end."

A small country, a lost world, the people we have met long dead, yet living still in the great onward flow of human steadfastness, determination and survival.

Siân James' novel needs no inflated length: it grows in the mind.

Stan Barstow

ONE

Catrin got down from the trap and looped the pony's reins over the post outside the station.

Ah, yes, a lovely girl, the porter said to himself as he watched her walking along the road to the main entrance. Paper-white brow, hair blue as a blackbird's wing. Who could describe the curve of her body as she walked? No one. Even ap Gwilym couldn't describe the body of a queenly young girl. Her body takes me from God, he'd said. Well, that was one way out of it. Her smile the five delights.

'She's on time tonight, Miss Evans,' he called out. 'Seven and a half minutes late at Ammanford. Your brother, is it? Good. He'll be home for the hay. One thing about these colleges, they give the boys a chance to help with the hay-making and the harvest. If they let them stop for the potato lifting as well, you'd get more of them going after an education. My poor sister's boy, now. He could pass any examination in the world, Miss Evans. He wrote a history of the three parishes for our Christmas Day Eisteddfod last year, and do you know what the adjudicator said about it? "This entry merits not a silver cup but a crock of gold." Aye indeed, a fine brain. But what would his mother do without him, that's the rub, isn't it?'

Catrin nodded her head sympathetically. It was a still, green evening. Even in the little station the scents of summer were all about her; grass and clover and hawthorn.

'Couldn't manage, Miss Evans, that's the truth of it. Five younger ones, you see. Couldn't manage. Even if they gave him one of these scholarships, they wouldn't give his mother a man in his place, would they?'

No one else on the platform. Sounds of summer in the little market town. Thrushes singing in the trees flanking the other side of the line. A horse clop-clopping lazily back to its stable. Children still out, playing and shouting on Llanybyther Road. 'Barley. Barley'. That was the only word she could hear distinctly. A dog barking somewhere.

9

'The knights used that word,' she told the porter. '*Barley*. In their tournaments.' She felt ashamed of her silence. So few people had time to talk to him. Only those marooned for hours between trains. His wife was dead.

It was the word the knights had used to call truce. It had survived for six centuries, its meaning virtually unchanged. The thought entranced her.

It didn't impress Mr Thomas, though, 'English Knights they'd be no doubt,' he said.

He took off his cap and scratched his head. '*Halen*,' he said. '*Salt*. A simple enough word, Miss Evans. A word that's been in our language since we first came to this island in prehistoric times, a Celtic word you might say. Now, *swllt*, *shilling*, the same stem but borrowed centuries later when the Roman legionaries tramped these hills. *Swllt* was salt money, wages. The same word arriving by different posts. There's a thought, now.'

Catrin nodded at him again.

'What name,' he said, 'do you give that animal of yours out there?'

'Bella'

'No, no, Miss Evans. I mean, what generic name do you give her?'

The train, under its neat puff of white smoke, suddenly appeared in the distance, saving Catrin from the necessity of venturing an answer.

'There he is,' she said, 'Tom.'

Her brother had the window down, was leaning out and waving at her.

'I'll go along and get his box,' Mr Thomas said.

'Where's Father, then?' Tom asked as he got out on to the platform. He looked about him as he brushed his lips against her forehead.

'I've come instead,' Catrin said. 'Won't I do?'

'But where's Father? He's always met me before.'

'Have you got a sixpence for Mr Thomas?'

'No, I thought Father would be here.'

'Haven't you got anything?'

'Welcome home, Mr Evans. Time for a bit of real work now, is it? Oh no thank you, Miss Evans. Not on any account in the world. I'll see your father in The Sheaf one of these days. "You owe me a pint, Mr Evans," I'll say to him, bold as cock robin. Don't you worry, Miss Evans. Now, I've put the trunk in the office. That's right, isn't it? You'll send for it tomorrow? Good. You'll be getting a motor-car soon, Mr Evans, I've no doubt. Emlyn John, Mr Ebenezer's son, you know, has got a beauty. Cost I don't know how much. The practice is going to the dogs though, they say. Well, what young man wants to be pulling teeth all day when he can be underneath an engine or thundering round the countryside, isn't it. He'll settle down soon, I dare say. No, I don't know what make it is, Mr Evans. Twelve horse-power though, he told me. I remember that. Twelve horse-power. Ah, but they don't tell you the nature and the spirit of the horse, do they? These men making their motor-cars in London, are they thinking about Mrs Gwynfor's Dolly or the Cribyn Flier, that's what I'd like to know. What sort of a horse have they got in mind? You find out, Mr Evans, before you buy yours.'

Bella trotted out smartly on the five-mile return journey, Tom now holding the reins.

He glanced at Catrin again. He knew she was considered good-looking, but it had never struck home to him until now. Now, as she sat next to him, staring in front of her at the road, she looked ... startling in beauty, splendid somehow, like a figure on the prow of a ship. Splendid and ... rather tragic. What was the matter with her?

'Where's Father?' he asked again.

'He's left.'

'What do you mean?'

'He's left us. Left home.'

'What do you mean? What the hell do you mean?'

'You know what I mean, there's no need to swear. He's gone off with one of his women.'

'One of his women. What do you mean? I'm ashamed to hear you say such a thing about your father. One of his women.'

'A special one, perhaps. Anyway, he's set up house with her and their baby. That's what they say. What's the matter with you,

Tom? Do you think I know nothing? I'm not a child. Don't you think I know my own father, what he's like?'

Tom stood up and touched Bella's flank with the whip. He couldn't wait to get home. To get hold of his father, to see him, question him.

'Where's he gone?'

'I don't know.'

'I thought you knew everything.'

'I think perhaps mother knows, but she hasn't told me.'

'How is mother?'

'Like she is when he's later than usual on a Saturday night. Of course, you've had time to forget the Saturday nights.'

Somehow they were quarrelling. They had rarely quarrelled.

'How long has he been gone?'

'Day before yesterday. I suppose he timed it to coincide with your holiday. Your vacation, I mean.'

'He'll be back.'

'I don't think so. I hope not. Oh let's get something settled.'

For three years at least, Catrin had known about her father, seen all the signs her mother had been too trusting to notice; how happy he was all day Saturday with Saturday night before him; the glazed, faraway look in his eyes on a Sunday; a man who had lost his road. She had known for years. If ever he and she were at a concert or meeting together during the week — her mother rarely went out at night owing to her indifferent health — she was aware, always of how he chose to sit as far away from her as possible, so that she shouldn't notice — but she did — how soon he slipped away. There were many, many tell-tale signs. For three years she had been waiting for the storm to break and now it had, and with any luck the air would be clearer.

'Edward's coming tomorrow,' Tom said.

Edward was his room-mate at Oxford, Edward Turncliffe. He had spent a month with them the previous summer.

'Oh no. You'll have to stop him.'

'I can't. He's on his way. He's cycling here. He's staying the night at Brecon or somewhere. I don't know where. I can't stop him.'

'Well, don't stop him then. Let him come. Life has to go on. Mother stays in bed. It may do us good to have Edward with us.

12

He'll help with the hay. He's good company. I'll be glad to see him anyway. Very glad.'

'Does everyone know?'

Catrin shrugged her shoulders. 'I suppose so. "When's he coming back, then?" they ask. "Hay's ready for cutting." '

'We'll start on it tomorrow.'

He shook the reins impatiently and Bella flicked her ears, a little hurt at the extra effort required of her on the last stretch.

'My God, what a home-coming. Why didn't you send me a telegram?'

'You might have thought it was bad news.'

'How can you joke at a time like this?'

They were silent for the rest of the journey home.

Hendre Ddu was a prosperous farm situated in mid Carmarthenshire. Rounded green mountains, where grass gave way to gorse and heather, encircled the farm, a fast-flowing river divided it from neighbouring land; the nearest village was three miles away, the nearest market town, five.

The front of the farm house with its beautifully proportioned windows and its elegant doorway, dated from the early eighteenth century; the back, the kitchens and dairies and the servants' bedrooms over them, from an earlier time, possibly Tudor; the fireplace in the best kitchen was huge and open to the sky, the beams blackened by centuries of smoke. The farm buildings spread out behind the house like a small village.

The farm had belonged to their mother's family, the Morgans, for generations.

Tom left the pony and trap to Catrin and walked through the rose garden to the front door.

Usually on his first evening home he was assailed by innumerable small pleasures; the beauty of the place, the warmth of everyone's welcome, all the sounds and smells he'd almost forgotten, the news and gossip which hadn't been considered important enough to be included in letters, the celebration meal. And whilst wishing to be a tower of strength to his mother – now, according to Catrin, lying prostrate in her darkened bedroom – disappointment at all he was going to miss made him feel like a surly schoolboy.

The house was quiet. He glanced briefly at the wide hall; the polished oak, the flagstones, the dark, glowing rugs. Then, catching sight of himself in the mirror over the fireplace, he hit himself sharply on the forehead. It was a gesture like someone tapping a barometer to make it settle.

He went upstairs to his mother.

Each time Catrin had been to see her, she had hardly turned her head or smiled or in any way acknowledged her presence, it was only Nano Rees the old housekeeper who could get a response from her, get her to drink some tea or take some gruel; Nano had been with her all her life. Yet when Tom went in she struggled to sit up, she patted her hair, straightened the top sheet, looked at him expectantly.

'Don't worry, Mam.' He held one of her thin hands. 'He'll be back. I'll get him to come back, don't you worry.'

'Did you pass your examinations Tom?'

'I didn't have any, Mam. Not this year. It's next year I do my Honours. There's no exam this year. Nothing to worry about.'

'I'd forgotten. You keep telling me in your letters. You look well, Tom. I'm glad you look so well. I think you've grown again. Have you?'

'I don't think so'

'You must be very tired after your journey'

'No, not a bit.'

'Oh, but you must be. Two changes and over an hour's wait in Cardiff and all the noise. Go down now, son, to have your supper. Nano is full of fuss waiting for you.'

'I won't have a meal unless you get up.'

'I can't possibly get up, Tom. I can't even walk to the bathroom.' She lay down again, weakly.

'Then I'll stay up here with you and have something on a tray.'

The thought of the sacrifice he was making made him feel virtuous.

He rang the bell and in a minute or two Catrin came in.

'Tell Nano I won't be having supper downstairs. Ask her to make me a few sandwiches and get her to send them up here. Beef, I'd like. The underdone bit by the bone. She knows the part I like.'

'Good. Beef. The underdone bit by the bone. Very good. The table's laid. Sewin, caught this morning by Davy Wern Isa, that's

14

the first course, jugged hare to follow because it's his lordship's favourite, I can't eat it, but who cares about that. Then, oh, then we have a choice; blackcurrant tart or raspberry and redcurrant puree. A few sandwiches, then?'

'Go down now, Tom, there's a good boy.'

'Not unless you come, Mam. You don't have to eat anything, just get dressed and sit at the table with us, that's all I ask. My first night home.'

'Tom, I can't.'

'I see a succession of little bedroom snacks before us. Edward will be here tomorrow night, have you told Mother? Edward Turncliffe. I'd just like to know, that's all, whether he'll be having sandwiches up here with the two of you and whether it's beef, slightly underdone, that he likes as well. I'd just like to know. Or will he want a bit more than that after cycling from Brecon or wherever it is, and even you perhaps after thirteen or fourteen hours on the hay.'

'Have you finished? I can't see...'

'Nano happens to be sixty-nine, that's all, and she's been slaving away for hours.'

'Do go down, Tom. Please.'

'I'll be up later, then, Mam.'

'I'll try to get up tomorrow, Tom, I really will. I'm not promising anything, but I'll do my best. Take the roses out, Catrin, they're giving me such a headache. Put them in the middle of the table downstairs, Nano will like that. Don't quarrel any more now, children. Tom is very tired, Catrin, after his journey.'

'I think this has been the worst evening of my life,' Tom told Catrin later, as he wished her good night.

He had eaten a very large meal with very little appetite, struggled to make small talk with Nano and the maids without mentioning the one thing on all their minds, endured an hour of his mother's silent suffering.

'You'll have plenty worse than this,' Catrin had said cheerfully. 'We'll make a man of you yet.'

TWO

The next morning, a little before six, Davy Prosser, the oldest of the menservants, called in to see Tom who was having his 'little breakfast' in the morning-room. (Little breakfast was a bowl of tea and a hunk of bread. Breakfast – porridge, eggs and bacon – was at nine.)

'Mr Tom, I'm not at all happy about Briony. Her cough is back and worse than ever, and her yield is down almost to half. Shall we get Parry over?'

It was a mere formality. Briony was one of the mothers of the herd, a valuable pedigree shorthorn. They both knew that the vet had to be fetched, and with no delay. The consultation, rapidly concluded, constituted a transfer of authority; it was the acknowledgment of Tom as the new master.

'How's Mrs Prosser, Davy? I shall be calling to see her one of these days. Not tonight, though. Mr Turncliffe – you remember my friend Turncliffe – he's coming later on today. Invited before I knew how things were here. Things are pretty bad here, aren't they?'

'Mr Tom, I don't ask questions.'

'You've got a right to, man. You've been here long enough.'

'Oh yes. Before your mother was married. Years before.'

'And I've always had a special regard for you. You know it very well. You were the one who taught me everything; how to ride, how to plough. And my Sunday School teacher as well, we mustn't forget that.'

'Aye indeed, come to think of it. You weren't so quick in the Sunday School, though, if I remember right. Never unruly, mind, but a bit of a yawn from time to time. Aye indeed.'

'Anyway, while I'm in charge here, as far as the stock is concerned, what you say goes.'

'That's it then. Well, we know where we are now. I'll send Glyn over to fetch Parry straight after breakfast. And I hope you'll come to see the Missis when you can. I'll be over at the hay-field myself

16

later on. What you cutting, Parc-y-Duar? Yes, That's what I thought. It's sweet as a nut.'

Rachel Evans sat up and drank her tea. Miss Rees had opened the curtains and given her the customary sermon. Counting her blessings was the text on that particular morning, with Mr Tom chief among them; strong, handsome, clever at book-learning, serious-minded, loving. If he had faults they were trifling ones like galloping through his allowance, which time would mend. Miss Catrin too, of course, only a bit sharp because of wanting to go to that college, and if it was up to her, Ann Rees, she should go, because nothing came of trying to change anyone's nature, and Miss Catrin's heart wasn't on the farm, that she could say. A beautiful home was next on the list. When Lady Harris had called last she had said she had never seen such exquisite china, not anywhere in the country. Exquisite. That was the word she used. And the linen. No one would credit the pairs of sheets; fine linen, best Egyptian cotton, flannelette, with pillow-slips and bolster cases to match. And tablecloths, drawn thread work, embroidered and plain damask, large and small, enough for Miss Catrin's bottom drawer and for her daughter's daughter. Next, the best farm in three parishes.

Rachel closed her eyes at that point.

'No more, Nano, no more now. I'll try to get up today, I really will. Edward Turncliffe is coming, isn't he, and I promised Tom to get up. I must make an effort. Women have been deserted by their husbands before this, I know they have, and without having you to look after them.'

Suddenly, she was in the old woman's arms and crying as she had not been able to do before.

'He's gone, Nano. He's gone. And he won't be back, will he, Nano?'

Miss Rees was now quite silent except for the occasional 'There, there. Come now. Come, come.'

But at last, since the storm showed no signs of abating, she spoke out again. 'We've managed without him before and we'll manage without him again.'

'I was never happy, never, never, till I had him.'

'You were happy enough before you ever saw him.'

'No. Don't say that. I wasn't. No.'

17

At last Rachel grew calmer. 'Where's Tom?' she asked then. 'Has he gone out already?'

'Yes. This half-hour or more.'

'Send him up to me, Nano, when he comes in for breakfast.'

She walked to the mirror on the dressing-table and sat in front of it. She looked ill, haggard, but not as bad as she'd expected. She felt much worse than she looked.

She was turned fifty but her hair was still thick and without a trace of grey. She brushed it, though without much strength, and put it up. She collected her things together to take to the bathroom. Everything was such an effort.

Rachel had never been a beauty nor had she ever possessed the liveliness which does instead. She supposed that would make acceptance of her position a little easier in time. She wouldn't have bruised vanity to contend with, at any rate. Only heart-break.

She was sitting by the open window in her bedroom when Catrin came in. 'Nano told me to tell you that Tom isn't coming in for breakfast. He's not going to stop. He's sent for coffee and toast. All the others are tucking in to ham and eggs and grinning like idiots. Shall I come to have breakfast with you instead?'

'I think I'll just have coffee and toast like Tom.'

Catrin kissed her mother, then hugged her hard. 'You look lovely, Mam, pretty and rested.'

'I'll make a handsome corpse.'

It was a family joke, what old Prosser, still straight and vigorous in his eighties, used to say. Catrin smiled. Then grew serious again as she noticed her mother's lips trembling.

'Coffee and toast, then,' she said.

Rachel wasn't swept off her feet into marriage at eighteen or nineteen as were most of her school friends, There was a serious-ness about her even at that age which the young men found off-putting. In her twenties she had settled down to being an old maid, to being her father's companion (her mother had died when she was five, she could hardly remember her), to useful work in the chapel and the local community.

She was twenty-nine when she received and accepted a proposal of marriage from a neighbouring farmer, Jim Reynolds, Dôl Goch, who had lost his wife the previous year. He was a fair bit older than she, but not old; nearer forty than fifty, and the arrangement seemed eminently suitable. The farmer had two children but they were away at school and seemed docile and well-mannered, unlikely to cause trouble. He was comfortably off, not rich like her father, but few people were in that part of the country. The farm house was pleasant enough, not quite what she had been used to, but it was assumed that Reynolds and she would return to Hendre Ddu when her father grew too old to manage it himself, and let Dôl Goch.

Rachel's father, old Griff Morgan, gave his blessing, though rather grudgingly, and the wedding was fixed for the following February, with a honeymoon in Bournemouth before the start of the ploughing.

In the months following her engagement Rachel became a different woman. She acquired a new poise, a spring in her step, authority in her voice. She put off the dark, spinsterlike clothes which, almost without realizing it, she had been wearing for the last few years, and instead adopted the bright, attractive clothes befitting a rich young woman about to be married.

It was at this time that she had met and fallen in love with Josi Evans, Cefn Hebog. She had been in love briefly, with most of the young men who had so rapidly married her friends, but this was the first time that her love had been reciprocated.

Josi was five years younger than Rachel, extremely handsome, dark as a gypsy and with a proud bearing. Indeed he did consider himself as good if not better than any man in the area, which was to say the world, and the fact that his father was a tenant farmer in one of the most inaccessible and barren one-horse farms in North Carmarthenshire did nothing to alter his opinion.

Rachel had been at the dressmaker's in Llanfryn choosing a pattern for a new dress and her father, who was to have picked her up at eleven, was late. Bored with the little dressmaker's company, and for some reason strangely restless, she had started to walk towards the King's Head where her father stabled his horse. Almost immediately it had started to rain quite heavily, so that she had hurried to take shelter in the covered courtyard of the inn. Josi, passing through on the way to get his pony, had noticed her there, a fine figure of a woman, her colour heightened by wind and rain, and with a flourish of his battered old hat had asked if he might take her into the lounge for a cup of tea. She had started to refuse but his eyes, such a vivid blue in the dark face, and the wide, friendly smile, had proved irresistible. 'Thank you,' she'd said. That's how it had begun. (Rachel's father was often to think, afterwards, how much it had cost him to haggle so long over the little Hereford heifers in the mart that morning.)

Josi knew who Rachel was. Perhaps that made him more ready to fall in love with her. But everybody who knew them at that time agreed that he had fallen in love with her and that he had remained in love for several months, perhaps a year or even two.

Her father, embarrassed about the promise to Jim Reynolds – though that was the least of his worries – taunted Rachel about breaking her word.

'But he never said he loved me,' she said, as though that excused everything.

'He wanted to marry you, girl, to unite two good farms, he wasn't after a free gift. Fancy words are for those who haven't anything else to offer.'

It was no good. Rachel would have Josi and the old man had to accept it.

But as he said afterwards, 'He didn't marry her for the farm, anyway, because he doesn't care a snap for it and never will.'

That's what ultimately damned Josi in his eyes. He could have had his bit of fun with the maids, or the pretty shop girls on market days, if he had cared for the farm, really cared for it. He could work as hard as any man, he was proud of his physical strength, proud of his prowess in driving a straight furrow and of his way with the horses. But he wasn't affected by the compound interest of farming. He was like a hired hand serving out his time till the next Michaelmas. Abiah Prosser and Davy Wern Isa, and even young Davy, liked to figure things out, they leaned on a gate with him and worried about the quantity of wild oats in the wheat, it had never been so bad, and whether swedes or mangolds would be more profitable for the March and April fodder, while his own son-in-law merely said, 'You tell me what to do and I'll get it done', as though that was some sort of virtue. There was something lacking in the man.

However, Griffydd Morgan kept his forebodings to himself. As for Rachel, she was conscious of nothing outside the closed, warm world of love.

THREE

Tom felt much better after his long, hard day in the hayfield.

His mother wanted him to be a lawyer; she had decided on it when he was quite a small boy – a lawyer was a gentleman – but he had never been wholly in favour of the idea, and it now struck him that if his father had really left for good, then he had an excellent excuse for throwing it over.

Tom was twenty-one years old, and for his age a remarkable realist. While some of his friends, no brighter than he, talked blithely of pegging away and getting a First, Tom knew that he would work fairly consistently and get a Third. He was also aware that he would never become anything but a rather inefficient country solicitor whose heart was in farming. So was the effort really worth it? Capital would have to be raised to buy a practice; one of the small farms would have to be sold, or at least some of the top fields. He'd rather keep them. He was a farmer like his grandfather, old Griffydd Morgan, and that's what he wanted to be. He derived positive pleasure from the feel of the sweat running down between his shoulder blades, pleasure, too, though not so easily defined, from the dark, gently-rising outline of the land.

He walked home with the other men, but found it difficult to talk to them and was angry with himself on that account. His father never had difficulty in talking to anyone. Why had he been sent away to school and to Oxford?

'I'm going to Derwen Pool tonight,' he heard young Glyn telling some of the others. 'Anyone coming?'

'I may, later on,' Tom said, knowing that he wouldn't go, and that the others would be embarrassed if he did. 'Good night, now.'

He took his boots off and went through to the parlour. 'Isn't Mother down?' he asked Catrin. He had set great store on her promise.

'She did get up this morning, but she had a letter by the second post which upset her again. Don't ask me what it was; she just read it and went back to bed. She won't say a word to me. Not even to Nano. One cup of tea, nothing else. You see if you can get anything out of her.'

'I'll have a bath first. No sign of Ned?'

'Not yet. What are we going to tell him when he comes?'

'I don't know. Let me find out what's in the letter; we'll decide afterwards. What's for supper?'

'Chicken soup. Lamb'

'Good.'

'Mr Tom.' Nano came out from the kitchen as he was going upstairs. 'I've made some beef tea for Mrs Evans, and if she won't have it I just want to say that I won't be held responsible; you'll have to get Doctor Andrews to see what he says to her. Three times I've taken up little bowls of this and that; egg custard, arrowroot, milk jelly and three times I've had to bring them down. She's had nothing all day but some coffee and a small piece of toast for her breakfast. Nothing else all day but a cup of tea. I just want to say that I won't be held responsible if she doesn't have the beef tea.'

'I'll see to it Nano, as soon as I've had a quick scrub.'

He kissed her, as though he was still a boy, and tore upstairs.

'Hello, Mam, I'm home,' he called as he passed her door. 'I'll be with you now.'

Stretching out in the warm bath, towelling himself dry afterwards, his spirits soared as they had on the hay-field earlier. He put on the clean shirt Nano had put out for him, his newly pressed trousers, his blazer. He had a different look on his face, though, as he tied his tie and brushed his hair: the dutiful son ready to see his mother.

He knocked on the door and went in. She turned her head to look at him but didn't smile. He sat on a chair at her bedside.

'Are you going to let me see the letter?' he asked, with no preliminaries.

'There,' she said, indicating with a slight movement of her head, the white envelope on the bedcover. Tom saw his Father's large, bold handwriting as he took out the single sheet of paper.

Dear Rachel,
We have been married almost twenty-three years and good years they've been for me. Now you have a grown-up son and daughter to

help you run your farm and to support you in every way. It's not for any young girl that I've left you, though you've been jealous of my very innocent attentions to them from time to time, but for a grown woman, nearly thirty, who has my child and who has no one else. She was the schoolmistress of Rhydfelen school. She gave in her notice, perhaps you remember, saying that she had to return to her family in Carmel. She has no family. At the moment we are in her aunt's cottage in Llanfryn. We shall soon be moving from the area.

I have very affectionate feelings for you and our children.

I hope Tom will bring me some of my clothes and other necessities.

I have taken £20 from the bank which I will pay back before Michaelmas. I'm sorry I couldn't tell you instead of writing. I meant to and would have except that you haven't been so well lately, so that somehow I couldn't get it out.

I don't know how to end this letter.

Forgive me if you can.

    Joshua Evans.

Tom sat at his mother's bedside, watching the lamp flickering, the blue outside the window turning blue-black, pitch-black.

Once, long ago, his pony had died. Suddenly. No one knew why. He was eight or nine. 'Dead?' he had shouted and screamed, banging his fists against his father's chest. 'Dead?'

'Do you remember when Blackbird died?' he asked his mother.

'You were very brave.'

'Brave? I cried myself to sleep for weeks and weeks. Don't you remember how I started wetting the bed?'

'Wasn't that when Grandfather died?'

'No, I didn't care a bit about that. You were so sure he'd gone to Heaven and it seemed such a good idea.'

'He was a good man.'

'I suppose so.'

'Go downstairs now. Edward will be here soon, surely. It must be half past ten.'

'Shall I take the letter? Show it to Catrin?'

'Isn't she too young to see it?'

'No. She knows things, it seems.'

'Show it to her, then. Read it to Nano too.'

'Right. You must take some beef tea, now, or she's going to have Doctor Andrews along in the morning.'

'Read it to her first, then. She'll be kinder about the beef tea afterwards, I can't keep anything down, Tom, I really can't.

Catrin read the letter, showing as little emotion as if it were a shopping list.

'Never,' she said at the end as if the total had been incorrectly reckoned.

'What do you mean?' Tom asked

'I'll never forgive him,' she said. 'Will you? How I wish Edward would come, the lamb will be dry, everything will be spoiled. The girls are in bed, and Nano should be, too.'

'I'll send her off now,' Tom said. 'You can see to the meal, surely.'

He went to the kitchen, the letter in his hand. Nano was sitting on the settle at the side of the range, her hands in her lap.

'You can take her the beef tea now,' Tom said. 'And then you get along to bed.' He found he wasn't able to read the letter to her after all. 'Father's written to say he's setting up house with Miss Lewis, the Rhydfelen school mistress. Baby, it seems. Take her the beef tea now, just a little. Spot of brandy in it, perhaps. Not so much that she'll notice.'

'Right,' Nano said, putting the little saucepan back on the fire and touching her eyes with her apron. It was true then, what people said.

'Why don't you have a little basinful with her?' Tom said. 'Spot of brandy. Do you good, too.'

'Right, right,' Nano said, wanting to be rid of him. He left her stirring the beef tea on the fire; muttering to it.

It was another hour before Edward arrived. By that time Tom and Catrin, too hungry to wait any longer, had had their supper. But so had he, he assured them, waving aside their apologies, so had he. While some good fellow at Llandre had mended his puncture, done an excellent job on it. And he'd had a wonderful trip; cloudless skies, memorable meals in roadside inns, the utmost courtesy from everyone. He couldn't stop smiling.

To Catrin, Edward seemed like a visitor from a distant, untroubled world. That's what it is to be English, she thought. Assured, self-confident, never brash, never on the look-out for insult, never brooding on imagined slights; victorious somehow, blessèd.

'I'll get you a basin of soup, anyway,' she said. 'It's a long way from Llandre. I'll get you a basin of soup and then I'll be off to bed.'

Edward was so full of good cheer, so high-spirited, so triumphant to have cycled from London in only five days, that Tom felt obliged to show him his father's letter. In a way he felt disloyal to be so fully exposing a family grief, but it was clearly going to be impossible to be with Edward without saying something, and saying everything seemed far less complicated.

His friend read the letter without a word and then handed it back.

'Right, then, soup,' he said when Catrin returned. 'That smells wonderful. Soup of the evening, beautiful soup. Thank you. We'll talk in the morning. I'm sorry to have kept you up so late.'

'Good night, Edward.' They shook hands.

Catrin was pleased, after all, that he had come. She'd almost forgotten the warmth of his presence. 'And now, no more the frost candies the grass', she said as she went upstairs.

'She doesn't seem to care a bit,' Tom said when they were alone again. 'Hard as nails, Catrin. Just as well, perhaps. My mother and the old girl are enough to put up with.'

'Hard as nails!' Edward said. 'I've never seen a girl so altered, the shadow of a shadow. Last summer she was.... Now she looks.... She's still beautiful, but.... Oh well, there's no use expecting you to notice, I suppose. This soup's wonderful. No one can make soup like Miss Rees. Tom, old chap, I'll only be able to stay a week or so this time.'

'That's quite all right. Just as well, perhaps. Things will be pretty miserable here, I'm afraid.'

'It's not that. Not that at all. I'd be glad to be with you through this business, very glad. It's not that at all. You see, it's Rose.'

Tom and Edward left the table and stretched out in a couple of armchairs with their pipes.

Tom wasn't really disposed to hear about Rose, who was Edward's fiancée, an active suffragette, and in Tom's opinion – he had met her half a dozen times – spoilt, headstrong, and altogether unsuitable for Edward who was easy-going and easily hurt.

'She's determined to be a martyr, old chap.'

'Will you be able to stop her?'

Edward took several puffs of the pipe which he had at last managed to light.

'No,' he said afterwards. 'But all the same, I think I should be around.'

Edward was two years older than Tom. He was fair-haired and tall, whereas Tom was dark and, though not short, several inches shorter than Edward. They had lodged together for two years. Neither had another close friend.

'Remarkable man, your father,' Edward said after a few moments' silence.

'Remarkable fool.'

Tom unfolded the letter again and re-read it. To his embarrassment, his eyes were suddenly full of tears. He turned his head as though to get more light from the big lamp on the table and blinked once or twice. 'Twenty-three years,' he said, when he was sure of being able to speak steadily. 'To throw it all away. A farm like this.'

'It's your mother's farm.'

'What's that got to do with it? When did she ever give any orders? Did you ever hear her give any orders? Say anything at all about running the farm?'

'No no. Only she told me several times it was her father's farm, her grandfather's, great-great-grandfather's. How many generations?'

'It was.'

'That's all I said old chap. It's her farm. It'll be your farm. But it wasn't his.'

'All right. All right. I take your point. But what's he got now? What's he got instead? He lived very well whether it was his farm or not. He never wanted for anything. My mother has always been stingy as hell towards me, but that's because of her damned Puritanism. She's so terrified that I'll become a gambler or a drunkard, or both, instead of a respectable lawyer. But she was never mean towards him.'

'But surely the fact that you can make that statement implies that the whole thing was on the wrong footing? "She was never mean towards him."'

'You're a fine one, you are,' Tom said at last. 'You've been preaching women's rights to me for two years; almost had me converted. But the first time you come across it in real life you find it rather distasteful.'

'I'm a mass of contradictions,' Edward agreed.

'My grandfather left his farm to his only daughter, entailed to me. What's wrong with that? My mother was five or six years older than my father. If she had died first, he might have married again and left it to another son or sold it.'

'I don't think he would have.'

'My grandfather probably wasn't the psychologist that you are.'

'Probably not.'

Tom managed a small smile.

'Things like this just don't happen in this part of the world,' he said, then.

'Things like this happen everywhere, from time to time.'

'I can't think of another instance. Not around here, anyway.'

'I don't suppose it would help you that much if you could.'

'Yes it would. One doesn't like to feel a freak. The family is sacred in these parts.'

'You make fun of the way your mother talks about Wales; no cases for the assize courts, "the land of white gloves", and so on; now you're as bad.'

'I suppose I am. It's shaken me, Edward, I can tell you that.'

'Of course it has. It's shaken me too. I feel more sorry than I can say.'

For a time they sat in silence. Then realizing how late it was getting, Tom rose to his feet.

'Are you mowing with me tomorrow?'

'Rather. "Killing the hay", as Miss Rees says.'

'I'll give you a call, then, at five, and we'll start on the slaughter.'

'I may not answer the call, old man. Not at five. The harvest is truly plentiful but the labourers are not all ready by five o'clock — I'll probably get up at about seven and then have an hour with Catrin, collecting the eggs. That's a job I'd leave home for, that is.'

'For God's sake, Ned, leave the girl alone this time. Leave her alone, for God's sake.'

'You mean her mind, I take it. A quick kiss and a cuddle, you wouldn't mind that?'

'Don't be an idiot, Ned. It's your subversive talk I'm afraid of. You know that very well.'

'We're both idiots, then.... What's the matter? I'm not serious.'

'I know that. No I was simply thinking about all the talking *we've* done in the last couple of years; enough for a lifetime, wouldn't you say? You know, I don't think I'll be coming back to Oxford next year.'

'We'll think about that again, old man. You can't make a decision like that after a long day in the hay-field. We'll talk again.'

Tom lit a small lamp for Edward and took him upstairs.

When he came downstairs he re-read the letter several times.

He had always idolized his father, had always felt such pride in his good looks and vitality, his unsought popularity everywhere; he was one of those people whose presence seemed to enliven any gathering; his laugh infectious.

If there was any singing anywhere, he would soon be singing loudly as anyone, making up words if he didn't know them; never at a loss.

He could remember listening to him when he was a small boy tucked up in bed, the sad, old songs, the break in his voice. *'Twas I who watched the ripening wheat, another has the harvest.* How desolate those words had made him, he'd had no idea that they referred to a woman, he was a farmer even then, it was the wheat he'd cared about, the precious harvest. But not his father, obviously.

He tried to remember Miss Lewis, Rhydfelen School, he'd seen her often enough at local gatherings. Small and insignificant he'd always thought her. A delicate, oval face, to be fair, a pretty way of holding herself; she certainly didn't look thirty.

And his father thought he loved her and their child. Tom felt a sudden pang of jealousy, a physical pain in his chest, to think that his father had now, perhaps, another son who would trail about after him. Catrin had never counted.

'Poor Mother,' he said to himself, 'if I can feel this.'

FOUR

Catrin found Edward still in the breakfast-room when she got down next morning. Miss Rees standing at the door keeping him company. It was a still, silvery morning, doves murmuring from the huge chestnut trees outside the windows.

'How is your mother today?'

There was a pause before Catrin replied. It was as though she was giving the question grave consideration. In fact she was savouring the moment; the smile, the friendliness, the June morning.

'She doesn't talk to me. It's only Nano she wants.'

'She thinks of you as a child, that's all. She's trying to protect you.'

Catrin looked at him gratefully, wondering if he could be right. It was a thing she hadn't considered.

'When may I go up to see her?'

Catrin looked towards Nano.

'She'll get up this afternoon,' the old woman said. 'Indeed I hope so.' She looked from one to the other, smiled at them both and left them. She could talk English wonderfully well, but it usually took her some little time to get used to an Englishman's English.

'Shall I pour you a cup of tea?' Edward asked.

'How nice that sounds. I don't think any other man has ever offered to pour me a cup of tea. It's always, "Let's have a cup of tea then, good girl".'

'Ah well, let's say it's my special privilege.'

He poured her a cup of tea and passed it to her. 'Shall I make you some toast? Boil you an egg? Clean your boots?'

Catrin smiled. She took a piece of crusty bread from the crock on the table and sprinkled sugar on it.

'How old are you?' Edward asked her. She had so many child-like ways.

'A year older than I was last summer.'

'Good. I'm glad that things are progressing in that orderly

30

manner. Some young girls are suddenly three or four years older between breakfast and dinner in these uncertain times.'

'I'm eighteen since January. It's true I feel much older, three or four years older than I did last summer.'

'You mean, because of your father?'

'Yes. Because of my father. I hate my father, Edward. I hate him.'

'But he's left home, so you should feel young and gay, Miss Catherine.'

'Do you really think so?'

'Of course not. I was being flippant just as you were being melodramatic.'

'I wasn't being melodramatic. I hate him. I've never idolized him the way Tom does; now I hate him. It's as simple as that. Why don't you believe me?'

'Finish your cup of tea and I'll come with you to collect the eggs.'

'Won't Tom be expecting you?'

'Probably. Do you hate Tom too?'

'No, I don't hate Tom. I'd like you better as a brother, though.'

'Why?'

'Because you consider me an equal. For instance, you'd think it was right and proper for me to go away to Art School.'

'Certainly I would. Doesn't Tom?'

They walked out, through the kitchen into the haze of early morning. Catrin put on her clogs and picked up the big oval basket from the bench outside the back door.

'It's going to be hot,' she said, squinting up at the sky. 'Oh no, Tom thinks I should stay at home.'

'What about your mother?'

'She doesn't say much; for or against.'

'I'll speak to Tom.'

'He won't listen. Girls stay home. That's how it's always been.'

As they walked across the farmyard to the hen-houses the cows were being turned out of the milking-shed and in single file were delicately picking their way towards the white gate which led to the water meadows. Edward stopped to watch them.

'Come on,' Catrin said. 'Any minute now, you'll be telling me how idyllic it all is.'

31

'I like cows,' Edward said, 'and I'm not going to pretend I don't because you're in a bad mood. I like the way they walk; their dignity, the lovely way they swing from side to side.'

'You can't swing from side to side and be dignified.'

'Cows can.'

'Do you like hens?' Catrin asked as they reached the hen-houses.

'Not as much as cows. Buttercup and Violet and Meadowsweet – is there really a flower called Meadowsweet? It's too good to be true – Fern and Primrose. I like cows, I really do.'

Edward held the basket while Catrin felt for the warm eggs, counting as she put them in.

'How idyllic it all is,' Edward said.

'I want to come to London. Do you think Rose would invite me to stay with her?' Catrin had turned and was looking at him so earnestly that he was forced to drop the bantering tone he usually adopted with her.

'I'm sure she would. She liked you very much. But I don't think Tom would want you to stay with Rose at the moment.' He spoke gravely and gently.

'He wouldn't stop me going on holiday. I don't mean now. I mean in September. After the harvest.' Even in the half-darkness, he was aware of the pleading in her eyes.

'Rose will probably be in prison by September.'

'Are you serious?'

'I am, unfortunately. Her plans are very different now from what they were when you met her last year. Now that she's twenty-one she's volunteered for what they call disruptive work, and that means stone-throwing or arson or any of the other crazy things.'

'Do you really mean "crazy things"?'

'No, I suppose not. I suppose I approve of almost all they do. All the same, I can't help wishing that Rose didn't feel obliged to do them.'

'I think she's wonderful. I'd never do anything if there was the slightest risk of prison attached to it. They're treated so badly there; I can't bear to think about it. I'd be perfectly willing to address envelopes or stand at street corners with leaflets, but nothing more than that.'

'That's just how Rose felt when she started. I remember her saying much the same a couple of years back. Now, she doesn't seem afraid of anything. The most terrifying thing is that she seems determined to suffer for the cause; she seems to long for a prison sentence as though it's a form of initiation she has to pass through.'

They'd collected all the eggs from the four hen-houses.

'Now the ones from the stable,' Edward said. He found he didn't want to talk much more about Rose.

'I haven't got many hens in the stable now.'

'What about Grace?'

'Yes, she's still there. Grace and one or two others.'

They walked over to the stable, a modern white-washed building standing next to the cow shed.

Grace was a large black hen who lived on terms of great friendship with Mabon, the biggest horse. She roosted on his back and laid her eggs in his manger. No one but Edward seemed to think the affinity particularly remarkable.

Catrin had a few words with Bella; the other horses were all out working; picked up a couple of eggs and scattered some corn on the floor. 'That's the lot, I think,' she said.

But, leaving the stable, Catrin didn't lead the way back towards the house but headed in the opposite direction, towards the old barn: a huge, mellow, half-timbered building now used as a cart house.

'It's like a church,' Edward said as they reached it. 'I wonder if it was ever a church?'

'No, just a barn. Barns were almost as important as churches in the old days, I suppose. It's beautiful isn't it? I've done several drawings of it; I'll show them to you some time.'

She stood just inside the massive door. 'This is where they used to do the threshing. The wagons came into the barn through that door, unloaded all the sheaves and left by this one. Then, in the winter, the sheaves were brought down from the far ends and threshed by flail, just here. It was the most back-breaking work on the farm, they say, threshing. And the grain was winnowed by being tossed in the air on a huge wooden shovel, we've still got one of them in the dairy, have you seen it and the chaff got carried away by the through draught from the doors, both pinned wide open as they are now.'

Edward, who had received all this information from Tom the previous summer, wondered a little at Catrin's desire to instruct him; she usually feigned boredom at anything to do with the farm.

'It's the oldest barn in the district; in the county, I think. Look at the beams. We've had people here from the museum in Cardiff. One man said the beams were six or seven hundred years old. Of course the lofts on either side are new, they're used to store grain and other food for the animals. You have to climb up to one of the lofts to see the roof arches properly.'

She left her basket of eggs in the pony trap and Edward followed her up the ladder. He had inspected the roof on his last visit.

'It's a superb barn,' he said. He hadn't felt so conscious of its beauty before. 'Medieval without a doubt. And you can still see the shape of the trees in those cruck beams. When were they felled, I wonder? Where did they grow? Quite near here you can be sure. No one would have wanted to carry those any distance.'

'We were forbidden to come up here when we were little, the ladder is too steep. But I did come up once; I was hiding from Tom and his friend.'

Edward realized that Catrin was about to tell him something important, that she had brought him up for that sole reason. He saw the pupils of her eyes dilate, with fear or some other emotion. He waited, feeling his heart beating.

'I saw my father up here with Maggie; she was a maid we had then. They were lying on some bags of grain in that corner over there. They didn't see me.'

The scene was as clear to Edward as though he'd been shown a photograph of it and he was startled and shocked by the strength of sexual desire it conjured up.

'What did you do?' he asked, trying to keep his voice steady.

'Nothing. Pretended I hadn't seen them. Got myself down the ladder again. Ran into the orchard and stayed there until it was dark, trying to understand it. Of course I understood it well enough on one level, but on another it seemed like a nightmare, all out of true.' He felt her distress. She turned towards him. Her mouth was close to his, her breath touched his cheek.

'And that was when you started hating your father? Is that what you're trying to tell me?'

'I wanted you to understand. You didn't understand. You thought I was being hysterical and unjust. Of course I forgot it in time; pushed it to the back of my mind; but lately, over the last few months, I keep remembering it again.'

'How old were you?'

'Nine or ten, I think.'

'Did you tell Tom?'

'Of course not. After a while Maggie left. I don't know why. Perhaps my mother suspected something.'

They climbed down the ladder without speaking. Edward was down first and he turned to help Catrin off the last steep step.

'Poor child,' he said.

'Yes.'

He wanted to comfort her, but dared not. The previous summer he would have put his arm round her shoulder in the most natural way in the world.

'Please get Rose to invite me to stay with her,' she said. 'Please. I want her to tell me what to do. I'll be swallowed up alive if I stay on here and I can't think where else I can go.'

'You'll have to stay with your mother for a time,' Edward said, his voice sounding quite harsh. He took the basket from her and they walked back to the stable and across the yard to the house.

Miss Rees met them at the back door. 'Wherever have you been, Miss Catrin? Doctor's here and he's been asking for you. Mr Tom must have got someone to ride over. Go straight up, now.'

She turned to Edward. 'Come for your breakfast, Mr Turncliffe. The men are almost finished.'

But Edward followed Catrin into the hall, watching her taking off her clogs and her print pinafore. She looked pale, pale and exhausted, blue shadows under her eyes, sweat on her upper lip. For the first time her beauty alarmed him.

He was going to marry Rose in a twelve-month's time. He loved her. When he was married and settled down he wouldn't be so affected by lovely young girls like Catrin.

When Tom came in, Edward had difficulty not to blurt out, I'm afraid I've fallen in love with your sister. But all he said was, 'Tom, I've got a thundering headache. I don't know that I'll be any help to you today.'

'No, you won't,' Tom said, glancing briefly as him. 'You tired yourself out with all that cycling.' He poured cream on his porridge and ate it swiftly.

'I'm still determined to quit Oxford,' he said, then. 'It seems the obvious thing to do, doesn't it. I'm needed here: you can tell that.'

Edward had stopped eating and was looking earnestly at his friend. 'I'll certainly miss you,' he said.

In a way, though, he felt pleased. He'd leave Hendre Ddu at the end of the week and try to put Tom and his beautiful sister out of his mind.

'I hope you'll let Catrin go to Art School if you're going to be here with your mother.'

Tom turned angrily towards him. 'Is that so important?' He wanted Edward to consider his decision, which was by no means as clear-cut as he'd made out.

'I've been talking to her this morning, that's all. Don't be offended, old chap. She seems rather desperate to get away. I think she's more affected by your father's leaving than you give her credit for.'

Tom grunted and didn't say another word until he'd finished his breakfast.

'Could you take Mr Turncliffe's coffee out into the garden?' he asked Sali, the second maid. 'I won't wait to have any more. Doctor Andrews will have a cup with him, perhaps, when he comes down.'

'I hope your headache will soon be better,' he said then, and left the room.

Edward went to sit in the rose garden in front of the house, glad to be on his own. In less than a minute, though, Miss Rees was out with him, standing against the white palings, her small eyes closed up against the sun.

'I'm afraid I tired myself out yesterday,' he told her. 'I'm not fit for mowing today.'

'Dear, dear,' she said in her high, sing-song voice. 'There's not a bit of need to bother yourself, Mr Turncliffe. We may be glad of some extra help with the turning but that won't be for a few days yet. The hay harvest has never been a serious affair, you know; even before the machines came, we never fretted ourselves over the hay. Now, the corn is a different matter, isn't it, the barley and the oats for the animals and the wheat for the house. If we left the wheat to the rain, the bread would be poor for a twelve-month and everybody suffering. But since the corn binder came, of course it's not the same job at all. Six or seven years ago we'd have as many as forty men cutting and binding, all the people of the little houses who had a row of potatoes on our land and a load of dung, would give so many days, and I'd have forty men to feed, let alone the wives and children.'

'Did you really? You must be glad those times are over.'

'Oh no, not glad; not glad. It's all different now, you see, the old machines taking us over. Years ago, all the cottagers were sharing in the harvest. It was a good feeling. It gave us a nearness somehow. Now, all we have in the *medel* is a miserable dozen.'

'The *medel* is the harvest supper, I suppose.'

'No, no, Mr Turncliffe, the *medel* is the reap, the men in the reap. And *medel rwymo* is the binding group, because there's cutting and binding as you know, and the debt for a row of potatoes and the dung was a day's cutting, but a day and a half binding. Do you understand me, now? All the cottagers had to have potatoes, you see, for the pigs, the bacon pig for the house and the porker for the rent. And the potato debt was paid in work for the harvest. Not the hay, of course. It was the women who turned the hay, the women did that for the buttermilk and the curds and whey they had from us, and the oat chaff for the bedding and so on. Do you understand me now?'

'I wouldn't like to write a paper on it, Miss Rees. It's bit complicated.'

'A bit complicated? At any rate, it's not as hard as the Welsh Miss Catrin set you to learn last year, is it? Do you remember any of it, say?'

'Very little, I'm afraid. Those mutations were beyond everything. *Pen Fy mhen. Ei ben.* The very devil.'

'Here's the doctor now,' Miss Rees said. 'I'll send out the coffee.' She went round the fence to the back door. Edward could hear her chuckling as she went.

Catrin brought the doctor to the garden, introduced the two men, then went back upstairs to her mother.

Sali carried out the coffee and poured it.

'How is Mrs Evans this morning?' Edward asked the doctor when Sali had left them.

Doctor Andrews took out a silver cigarette box and handed it to Edward.

Edward had an extraordinary feeling of being outside himself, witnessing two men talking over their cups of coffee. It's a bad business, the doctor would say, shaking his head a little. The other would nod.

'It's a bad business,' the doctor said.

Edward nodded his head sympathetically.

'You're conversant with the situation, I take it?'

Edward nodded again.

He couldn't keep his mind off Catrin. He thought of the shape of her breasts through her print dress, her cream skin, all softness. Why hadn't he put his arm around her and kissed her? What was the harm in a kiss? He imagined the touch of her lips, her breath on his.

'It's a matter of class,' the doctor was saying. 'If Joshua Evans was a gentleman the matter would be settled differently. The woman and child would be provided for, there's no shortage of money, and poor Mrs Evans none the wiser. That's the way things have always been done.'

Edward nodded again. Rose and he were respectably married and Catrin being provided for. He picked her up and laid her on the red sofa of their love nest. Her lips opened as he kissed her and the pupils of her eyes dilated. He'd never seen eyes that were truly green before, green as the sea, stormy.

'Still,' Doctor Andrews said, pushing his coffee cup away from him and stubbing out his cigarette, 'we can't sit here all morning, can we, putting the world to rights. I've enjoyed meeting you, Mr Turncliffe.'

Catrin appeared at the door as the doctor was leaving. 'I'll come to Llanfryn with you, Doctor, if that's all right. Are you going straight back?'

'It'll be a quicker way to get the medicine and a few other things that Miss Rees wants,' she told Edward. 'Doctor Andrews has a motor-car. I'll get a lift back from Arthur, Ty Croes.'

After she'd gone, Edward sat down again in the garden. It was already hot, too hot. The scent of orange blossom came to him from somewhere, and it was as heavy and artificial as the perfume counter in one of the Kensington stores. The bees climbing into the foxgloves suddenly seemed like old men stumbling into their clubs, and too-sudden love was only lust, he was better without it. Rose was the daughter of his father's business partner and oldest friend;

their marriage would be suitable in every way, he liked her, loved her, wanted to look after her, to protect and cherish her. But....

'Catrin.'

At first he thought he had spoken aloud, then realized that Rachel Evans was in the garden. He rose to his feet and went towards her. They shook hands.

'I'm so sorry to find you unwell,' Edward said. 'Catrin has gone to Llanfryn with the doctor. May I get you some coffee or some tea? Or anything at all?'

But Miss Rees was already out again with a straw hat and a cushion and a shawl.

'Mrs Evans, bach, you're looking much better, indeed you are. Almost your old self again. Mr Tom will be so pleased to see you up, he was disappointed yesterday, wasn't he, Mr Turncliffe? Now have a cushion behind your back, that's right, and you'll need this as well. Oh yes, you will. You've come straight from bed and it's light as a feather. Catrin went with Doctor Andrews to get the medicine and she's bringing a bit of sea fish as well for your dinner. Now I'll fetch you a little glass of egg and milk. Will you take some egg and milk, Mr Turncliffe? It's an excellent thing for a headache, or would you prefer barley water? You must have something to keep Mrs Evans company, isn't it.'

'We'll both have some of your lemonade, Nano, a bit later on. You can go now. I know you've got too much to do as usual. Do sit, Mr Turncliffe. I hope you'll be able to stay a good long time with us. It's wonderful for Tom having you here, he gets very lonely on his own.'

They sat and talked and afterwards sipped lemonade as though it was a perfectly ordinary morning.

After dinner, Edward helped with the mowing.

FIVE

They finished cutting Waun Hir by seven, so that all the men knocked off at a reasonable hour.

Rachel Evans sat at the supper table with Edward and her children that evening, the three young people trying not to notice how little she was managing to eat. Instead of eating, she talked. About the farm, about the old days when her grandfather had drained the marshland bordering the river, put the stony heathland, 'The Top', under the plough, and planted all the trees. 'Morgans have lived here ever since the old house was built,' she told them. 'Search the church records and you'll find an Elys Morgan in Hendre Ddu in 1637, a Llwyd Morgan afterwards, another Elys after him. This part of the house was built in 1741. Most of the furniture, made by local craftsmen, came at the same time; this table, these chairs. The clock too. This dresser and the one in the front kitchen.'

She seemed feverish, talking compulsively, no one able to stop her. Edward broke in to ask appropriate questions which Tom tried to answer, but his mother wouldn't be deflected; she insisted on answering every time, answering fully, elaborating and then repeating herself.

They were all relieved when the meal was over and she ready to go back to bed. Catrin went upstairs with her and later went out to the kitchens to help Nano and the girls with the vast quantity of washing-up they had after the men.

Edward and Tom decided to take a walk as far as Pen Bryn.

It was a fine, cool evening, the colours just fading from the hills, the sky full of pale yellow clouds. The river sounded close and full.

'I've stood here with him hundreds of times,' Tom said. He kicked the lowest bar of the gate as they reached it.

Edward sighed. He was thinking of Catrin, imagining her there with them, imagining her arm brushing against him.

'He always said he didn't care for views. He always said he hated the land. "Go to London," he was always telling me, "there's no bloody farms there". But he stood here all the same, night after night.' Tom kicked at the gate again, though more gently. 'He was a fine figure of a man,' he said. He spoke as though his father was dead.

'He was,' Edward agreed, suddenly feeling grateful to the begetter of so much beauty. He thought of Josi Evans, dressed always with some flamboyance in corduroy and flannel and tweed; essentially a countryman, he couldn't imagine him translated to the city. Whereas Catrin's looks would fit her for any life she chose. He saw her in London society; graceful, stylish, slightly bohemian; a beauty anywhere, by any standards.

'Even at his age, he turned heads,' Tom said. 'Even last Easter in the ploughing competition, I couldn't help noticing how the women looked at him. It's more difficult for someone like that to keep on the straight and narrow. It's easy for other men to preach. They haven't had the temptations. Roderick the minister, now; a few wisps of sandy hair, no eyebrows, very little chin, what does he know about temptation?'

'He called to see your mother this afternoon? Mr Roderick?'

'Yes.'

'She finds him helpful?'

'Yes. She said he prayed for us all. She likes that sort of thing. There's no harm in it.'

'Was Catrin there?'

'I shouldn't think so.'

'She isn't religious?'

'I honestly don't know. She doesn't feel much about anything, that's my opinion. I know you think otherwise.'

Tom's despondency suddenly took on an aggrieved edge. 'You may not have noticed it, Ned, but Catrin's getting too pretty by half. I don't mean that she's beautiful like some women you see around, Professor Warren's wife, for instance, but she's eye-catching in a way that makes me worry about her. To be perfectly honest, that's one of the reasons I don't want her going away to college. One simply doesn't know what she might get up to.'

'Your parents might have said the same about you and stopped you going up to Oxford.'

'Men can look after themselves.'

'You just said they can't. Your father couldn't. You just said so. To tell you the truth, I don't feel too confident about you. On the other hand, I think Catrin is quite capable of looking after herself.'

'I'm not so sure. Why can't she just stay home till she gets married? What good will college or Art School do her? She'll get married eventually. You can tell by looking at her that she's not going to turn out a blue-stocking.'

'Who is there for her to marry if you keep her here?'

'There's no shortage of young men here. What's wrong with a farmer? I'd have no objection to any go-ahead young farmer as long as he was going to inherit sixty acres or so. And there's a teachers' training college at Llanfryn. According to Nano, those students keep things pretty lively around here. She was talking about the maids but I can't see that Catrin need be left out. She went to evening classes at the college last year; History and Welsh literature, I think. What's wrong with a teacher? Mother would help them along. Then there's Doctor Andrews. He's very attentive.'

'Isn't he married?' Edward felt a sting of jealousy as he thought of the doctor's dark good looks and assured manner.

'He's a widower. No children. Good practice.'

'He's much too old for her; he must be almost forty. I don't like him either. I know I've only met him once, but I don't like him.'

'Why not? He's a very clever chap. Very well thought of.'

'He's too smooth.'

'Smooth? John Andrews? I've always considered him a pretty rugged sort of character. Anyway, Catrin likes him.'

'Let her go to Art School. Her heart's set on it. If she was keen on Doctor Andrews she wouldn't want to go.'

'What about me? What company would I have if she was away? She's someone to argue with, if nothing else. Someone to tease.'

'But in no time at all you'll get married, see if you don't. There'll be no end of girls throwing themselves at you.'

Edward had expected a smile, but even in the fading light he could see Tom's look harden.

'You were lucky, Ned,' he said. 'You were free to choose. I'll have to marry for money. I saw Charles our solicitor this morning and he's warned me that our financial position isn't what it was. My father's heart wasn't in farming. It's lucky that mine is. All the same, I'll have to marry money. I can only think of one suitable candidate and she's about thirty. It's a daunting prospect.'

'What will your father do, Tom? Have you any idea?'

'Not really. I've written to ask him to meet me at The Sheaf in Llanfryn on Saturday evening to arrange a few things; getting his stuff to him, for instance, I don't really know what he wants. Dick Charles had heard he was trying for a job in some farm in Cardiganshire. I suppose it'll be better if he moves away from here. Did you hear that Catrin saw his little schoolteacher in the chemist's this morning?'

'Good heavens, no! What happened?'

'Nothing, really. No confrontation. Catrin saw her, that's all she said.'

'It must have been terrible for her.'

'No. I tell you, Catrin doesn't feel it like I do.'

In bed that night, Edward was too hot, too excited to sleep. Last year he had enjoyed a month's working holiday at Hendre Ddu and had envied Tom's carefree home life. Catrin, he'd considered a lovely bonus, the beautiful sister thirsting for the kind of talk he excelled at; classicism and romanticism in literature and art, absolute standards of criticism, the nature of God, ideas of immortality. She had flattered his ego and stimulated his senses. He had been drawn back, though Tom's invitation hadn't been pressing; he had suggested a walking holiday in Scotland at the end of September, had warned him that a second holiday in Hendre Ddu would be an anti-climax.

Yet he had come. He wondered whether Catrin, even last year, had exerted a greater influence on him than he had cared to recognize. Whether it was she, in fact, who had brought him back.

This year, she disturbed him so much that he was forced to re-examine all his assumptions about love and marriage. He desired Catrin, ached for her, couldn't stop thinking of making love to her. He couldn't look at her face without imagining her strange green eyes opening wide in surprise against the passion of his kiss. The buttons on her blouse, the frill of her skirt, her small feet, even in the clogs she wore on the farmyard, excited him so much that he had to look away. Feelings he had previously only experienced at the music hall or when seeing girls he would have been ashamed to talk to, now troubled him every minute, and though his first impulse was to leave Hendre Ddu as quickly as possible and return to London, to Rose whom he loved without embarrassment, the disaster of Mr and Mrs Evans's marriage seemed to serve as a warning that sex was not to be so easily dismissed.

Doctor Andrews had shown no surprise at the fact that Josi Evans had a mistress and child, only that he was leaving home for them. Was marriage, then, as frail an institution as it had been in Victorian times, when the wife was worshipped and the husband's lust satisfied in the brothel, or in an alternative establishment if he were rich enough? Wouldn't he himself be heading in that direction if he married Rose whom he loved, yes, but who had never excited him as Catrin did? He had often thought longingly of marriage with Rose, their close domesticity, but he had never imagined undressing her, seeing her white and naked under his hands.

Wasn't it possible to find love and passion in one woman? Catrin, he felt sure, was as tender and warm as she was intelligent and beautiful. Tender and warm. Why should he try to deceive himself; she looked like someone who would love passionately, that's what he meant. Dear God, he was mad for her.

The right thing to do, surely, was to break off his engagement to Rose, however much distress it would cause them both and their families, and to choose again where his body worshipped as well as his mind. 'With my body I thee worship. With my body I thee worship.' He repeated the words like a spell. 'With my body.'

He got out of bed and went to the window. It seemed so simple. What could prevent it? He would break off his engagement to Rose – it would mean less suffering in the long view – and return a free man, and ask Mrs Evans, Mr Evans if he could be contacted, for their permission to court Catrin, to begin his life again, to be re-born.

That's what he would do, God help him, that's what he would do. He opened his window wide to the smell of the orange blossom. He could hardly bear to go back to bed.

He slept at last, and when he woke it was some time after eight; Tom would have been out for hours, he liked to mow while it was cool, while there was still dew on the grass. He got dressed and went downstairs, the excitement and ardour of the previous night still persisting.

'I was just coming up to call you, Mr Turncliffe,' Miss Rees said as he opened the morning-room door. 'There's a telegram come for you, look.' She held the yellow envelope a good distance from her stout, wholesome body as though fearing contamination from it.

'And I hope it's not bad news,' she added, as he took it from her and opened it.

Please come home. Rose in trouble. Mother.

'I have to return to London at once, Miss Rees.'

'Not illness is it, I do hope?'

'Not illness, no. Just some tedious family trouble.'

'There's a lot of that about this year, yes indeed. You'll go by train I suppose, Mr Turncliffe?'

'Yes, by train.'

'That will be the ten-fifteen, then. I'll cook your breakfast now and make you some sandwiches and Miss Catrin will take you to the station in the trap. What a pity Doctor Andrews isn't coming this morning, he'd have you there in no time. Poor old Bella is past her prime now. I do hope Mr Tom will buy a big shiny motor-car soon, then we'll all go to chapel in style, isn't it. Will they take your bicycle on the train, say?'

'They would, but I think I'll leave it here for the time being.'

'Well, that's good. It's a champion old bicycle. Glyn and Daniel ride it around the clos, I hope you don't mind. Miss Catrin said you wouldn't mind. We're only young once, aren't we. And not always once in these parts. "A man at eight", my father used to say.'

'I don't mind in the least, Miss Rees. They're welcome to borrow it. Is Miss Catrin out getting the eggs?'

'Finished, Mr Turncliffe. She's upstairs with Mrs Evans now but she'll be down soon, I dare say. Miss Catrin is getting a very pretty girl, have you noticed it, now?'

'I have indeed. Very beautiful.'

'It's a pity for a beautiful girl to go away to college, don't you think so, Mr Turncliffe?'

'No. It'll be just the thing for her, I think.'

'But don't you think she'll find herself a very good husband if she's as beautiful as you say.'

'There's plenty of time for that.'

'But is a college education necessary for being a good wife and mother?'

'It's not necessary, Miss Rees, not at all. It's like that orange sauce you make with the baked ham, it's not necessary because your ham is the best in the world without it. But it's good all the same.'

Miss Rees was silent for a moment, standing with her arms folded demurely over her snowy white apron.

'I've noticed that you think Miss Catrin is very beautiful.'

'I haven't made any secret of it.'

'I've got nothing against secrets, mind, nothing at all. Anyway I like a man who appreciates his food, I will say that, and I don't mind a bit of a secret now and again. You shall have some of my best fruit-cake after your ham and eggs this morning, the one I keep for Lady Harris, it will last you the day, that will. Mrs Evans will be very sorry to hear that you're going back. She was worried that you weren't sleeping so well last night; she heard you opening the window and walking about. But I said, Mrs Evans bach, he's the age for sitting at the window in the moonlight and what harm will it do him, he'll sleep the sweeter in the morning. Pity the old telegram had to come. Yes indeed.'

At last Miss Rees left him and he stood at the window alone, pressing his forehead on to the cool glass, listening to the sadness of the ring-doves in the trees encircling the house.

He wondered whether the telegram would affect the resolve he'd made the previous night. What sort of trouble was Rose in? Was she in prison, being denied bail? Had she been injured in a skirmish with the police? It was an effort to think of such things.

He'd always considered himself old for his years. An only child, he had spent most of his childhood in the company of adults. At fourteen he had had meningitis and had lost two years of school, which was the reason he still at university at twenty-three. Yet, that morning, he felt very immature; much too young to be of any help to Rose – why did they ask it of him? When all he wanted was a summer of being eighteen with Catrin.

Tom came in for breakfast. He'd already heard the news from Miss Rees. Edward handed him the telegram and shrugged his shoulders. 'I hope to get back before the end of summer,' he said.

'You'll be very welcome,' Tom said. 'Write and let me know if there's anything I can do. I wish you didn't have to go.'

They sat down to breakfast. Catrin didn't join them; as usual taking hers upstairs with her mother.

46

Immediately after breakfast, Edward went to his room to do his packing. He carried down his rucksack and the trunk which had been sent by train, left them in the hall, and went to the kitchen to find Miss Rees. He asked her whether he might go back upstairs to say goodbye to Mrs Evans; he dreaded that she should be feeling worse, so that Catrin wouldn't be able to drive him to the station.

'Mrs Evans is coming down now,' Miss Rees said. 'And I've packed you a dozen eggs and a pound of butter, look. For your mother. And you can tell her that you collected the eggs yourself.'

She pushed the brown paper parcel into his hands; her eyes were mischievous slits in her large, old face.

Rachel Evans and Catrin were already in the morning-room when he got back from the kitchen. Mrs Evans took his outstretched hand and motioned him to the chair at her side. 'You'll have to harness the pony, Catrin,' she told her daughter. 'Even Davy is out this morning.'

'Mr Turncliffe,' she said as Catrin left them, 'you do my son a power of good and we all hope to see you again soon.'

Edward thanked her and said he would be back before the end of the summer.

'Have you heard that Tom isn't returning to Oxford?'

'He mentioned it. I wasn't sure that it was definite.'

'I believe it is. Do you think he's made the right decision?'

'I'm sure he'll give the matter plenty of thought and reach the right decision.'

'If Tom remains at home, then I shall have no objection to Catrin going away to college. She tells me that Miss Fletcher, your fiancée, has offered to keep an eye on her if she should manage to get to that Chelsea College of Art she talks so much about.'

Edward was taken aback so that his only response was a slight bow. After a few seconds, though, he was able to say, 'It's an excellent school, I believe. One of the best in the country.'

Mrs Evans turned and looked full into his eyes. 'Oh, Mr Turncliffe, I used to think London was a terrible place, a wicked place, but now I know that this place and every place is terrible and wicked too, so why should I try to keep her here.'

After the sudden outburst, she sat up straight again and drew a deep breath. Then she consulted the little gold watch she wore on a chain around her neck.

'I mustn't delay you,' she said. 'Come again if you can put up with us.'

Edward took her hand, pressed it, and left the room. He was surprised and also moved that she had so fully exposed the raw edges of her suffering.

Catrin was already sitting in the trap when he went out to the yard. He put his luggage in the back and went to join her on the seat at the front. She was wearing a cream, lacy blouse and a dark skirt. She looked different; older, more self-assured. Edward wished she was in one of her usual bright print dresses.

Miss Rees and the two maids were at the back door to wave them away.

They drove up the narrow, tree-lined drive into the tree-lined road.

'You're a ruthless one, and no mistake,' Edward said at last, breaking the green silence of the morning. 'What's all this about Rose promising to keep an eye on you?'

'I have to get away, Edward, I must. I don't do my mother any good. It's only Tom and Nano she wants. It'll be worse than ever now that Father's left home; we'll live in a sort of half-mourning all our lives. I suppose I could escape by getting married, but I don't want to be a little black wife here in the country. You don't know what it's like, you've only been here on holiday. Nobody does anything interesting. Nobody seems to want to do anything but go to chapel and the weekly chapel meetings. The singing festival and the local eisteddfod are the social highlights of the year. The ploughing contest is what we lose sleep over; they think I'm unnatural because I don't get excited about it. Our minister was publicly reprimanded because he took his seven-year-old son to the circus; it's the only thing I've ever respected him for, it's not that I approve of circuses, but at least it's better than taking a child to a prayer meeting. But what is there for *me* to do? I'm not living, I'm existing. I've got to break out, I've got to, or I'll go mad.'

'And yet you can't forgive your father,' Edward said, realizing even as he said it that he had made a monumental blunder.

48

And indeed Catrin stared at him unbelievingly for a second and then struck him hard on the cheek. She reined in the pony. 'You can get out and walk,' she said. 'You'll have time if you hurry. I'll send the trunk after you.'

Edward had been so looking forward to the drive, and was so thrown by this turn of events, that he, too, lost control of himself. He grabbed her by the shoulders and pulled her towards him and kissed her hard on the mouth. Only a moment she resisted, then her lips opened for his kiss and she was kissing him back. Their eyes were open and amazed as they went on kissing each other without a word. Soon his hands were opening the buttons which had so enchanted him and pulling aside skirt and petticoat.

'Let's go into the field,' he said, his voice parched and rough.

'No.' She was crying now and re-arranging her clothes. 'No.'

'You must go,' she said. 'Take Bella and leave her outside the station with Mr Thomas. Say I felt faint. I do feel faint. I do. I'll walk on later. Please go. Please.'

Edward, too, was horrified by what had happened. All he had dared hope for was to sit near her for the duration of the journey and to hold her hand and perhaps kiss her cheek at parting.

'I'm sorry,' he murmured over and over again. 'Dearest, I'm sorry. Don't make me go. Don't make me leave you. Tell me you forgive me. Oh my dear, say you forgive me.'

'We both need forgiveness,' Catrin said at last. Suddenly she seemed calmer than he. She shook the reins and drove on letting the tears dry on her face.

'I love you, Catrin, I've known it since the moment I arrived. I think I knew it last year. I shall break off my engagement to Rose. When you come to London, I shall visit you every weekend and take you to art galleries and museums. Will you be my sweetheart, Catrin? Oh, promise me that you will.'

His voice had taken on a hypnotic quality, pleading and tender, but somehow sure of success.

'I don't know,' she said at last. 'I don't know what will happen.'

They drove on in silence until they could see the little town spread out before them. The morning was cloudless.

Catrin turned into the narrow side road leading to the station. Edward took his watch from his pocket. 'We've still got half an hour,' he told her.

But Catrin refused to wait with him in spite of all his pleading. She gave him her hand for an instant, then turned and left him without a backward glance.

She let Bella choose her own speed on the journey home. It was very hot. 'I don't know what will happen,' she kept repeating desolately.

Edward had almost reached Paddington before once thinking of Rose. He had dwelt only on the encounter with Catrin; his emotions gradually changing from shame to delight and excitement. Some of the time, he simply couldn't believe what had happened, he had to reconstruct the whole scene, step by step, word by word, from their departure from the house to the point when she had turned blazing eyes on him and struck him.

He wrote her several letters, varying in tone from first to last.

I hope you can forget the inconsiderate way I behaved this morning. Believe me, nothing of the sort shall happen again to mar our courtship. Please write to me to tell me you forgive me.

My apologies and regrets were false. How can I regret the most beautiful moments of my life? I shall never forget how we looked at each other and strove for closer closeness. I shall never be able to stop thinking about what happened. Please write to me and tell me you love me as I love you.

Green-eyed Kate, half girl, half woman, tall and white-skinned under my hands, whose empty clogs I worship, whose skirts I touch in a fever of longing, grant me your peace.

He tore up all of them. None of them expressed the amazed joy and hope in his heart.

SIX

When Josi Evans was a boy, he was a prize-winning singer. He had tramped or cadged lifts to every eisteddfod in the four parishes, usually winning first prize, a half-crown in a gaily-coloured satin bag; once a 'big' crown. As a young man his voice had not been so predictable, though he still competed when it was, as he said, 'steady', winning twice or three times the half-guinea baritone solo and once the silver cup in the open class.

Since his marriage it was, of course, beneath his dignity to compete, though he went to several meetings throughout the year, often being asked to chair and always contributing handsomely to the funds.

To Josi's disappointment, Tom had no sort of voice so that getting him to sing publicly was a lost cause; he was only a passenger in the chapel choir. But Catrin sang like a bird and her father was dismayed that Rachel was against her competing even in their local eisteddfod.

When she was twelve years old, though, and had gone from the little private school at Henblas to the county grammar school at Llanfryn, she announced one day that she had been chosen to represent her house in the St David's Day eisteddfod at school. Since honour points only were awarded, no money prizes, Rachel was unable to object, and Josi was delighted and determined that his daughter should acquit herself well.

'Miss Lewis, Rhydfelen school, would train her,' Nano had said. 'They say she's very good.' And though Josi would have preferred a qualified singing teacher, there were only three weeks to the eisteddfod, so that he decided to ride over that very day to catch the schoolmistress before she left school.

He was outside on the dot of three-thirty; in time to see the little ones, capped and scarfed and gaitered, running home through the bleak February winds. The big children followed; several of the boys crowding round offering to hold his horse. 'Too cold for you,'

51

Josi said, 'run off home.' He distributed some ha'pennies, tied the horse to the post by the gate and walked up the path.

He opened the outside door, stopped a moment in the porch sniffing the familiar smell; sweat and chalk and damp clothes, then tapped at the classroom door.

Miss Lewis was sitting close to the stove, lacing her outdoor boots. She greeted him warily. She knew him by sight; knew who he was.

The meeting did not go well. Miriam Lewis had only recently been appointed schoolmistress to the little one-teacher school, and was finding that there were too many people – members of the local gentry, ministers of the various chapels – who thought they had a right or duty to help her run the school.

Josi explained his errand.

She said that she trained only children from her own school. She was tired and cold and Dewi Williams, a great bully-boy of thirteen, had been difficult all day.

She regretted her refusal as soon as Josi had left. From a safe distance she watched him striding down the path and getting on to his horse. If he had been just a little less sure of himself, just a shade less handsome, she would have been more courteous.

She was insecure, that was the trouble. Born and bred in uncompromising poverty, pride had been the only luxury; had remained the devil at her elbow.

Her mother, a widow who had lost her tied cottage along with her husband, had brought her up in a tumbledown shack, just about managing to keep them both alive by going out washing and scrubbing floors. Miriam, dark-skinned and under-sized, had led a solitary life, no brothers and sisters, unwilling or unable to mix with other children.

When she was about twelve, approaching school-leaving age, the squire's wife, at the Christmas celebrations in the church hall, noticing her because she had received her gifts of an orange and a three-penny piece with a sullen thank you and no curtsey, had asked Ifan Jenkins the schoolmaster whether she was 'all right', wanting to know, presumably – she acted as an unofficial employment agency – whether she was fit to go into service. He, having other plans for her, had shaken his head.

He knew how to get round her. While the other children were chanting the names of the rivers and mountains of Canada and Central America, he would take her aside and they two would work on Euclid and Geometry and Matriculation English, and then she became an ordinary, contented child, would even smile from time to time. If she had been a boy he would have moved heaven and earth and the county education authority to get her a scholarship to Oxford or Cambridge. As it was, he had gone to see her mother and begged her to let her have another year at school as an assistant uncertificated teacher.

'She's got a remarkable head on her,' he'd told Mary Lewis, and she had been amazed; she had always considered her poor Miriam not quite twelve to the dozen; it was only idiot children in her experience who devoted so much time to rearing fledglings and singing and crying over dead hedgehogs and mice. Still, to be a teacher was a fine and grand thing, and if Jenkins the school said her daughter would make a teacher, then she would take in more washing, scrub more floors to keep her at school a bit longer; of course she would. And with Lisi Jenkins so kindly offering to get her the material for a suit and a winter cape, it was only the boots she'd have to worry about; a teacher, even a fourteen-year-old assistant, uncertified one, couldn't go to school bare-footed.

So Miriam hadn't had to go into service.

Not that she had had it easy. After her breakfast of bread and tea, she would walk, summer and winter, the three miles to school, getting there by seven-thirty, so as to have an hour's tuition from Mr Jenkins, analysing and parsing, precis and composition, model drawing, music, mathematics, literature; English, Welsh and Burns; they did a day's work in that hour, then a cup of tea from Mrs Jenkins and she was ready to meet her pupils at ten to nine.

Her double life, studying and teaching, had gone on for four years, until at eighteen she had gone to Swansea to be examined for her teacher's certificate.

There again, she had nearly lost everything to her pride.

The last exam – she had been at it for three days – was music. The theory paper had been easy enough. Afterwards, she had had to submit to an oral examination. Some simple piano pieces, she sat with her back to the examiners, trying not to laugh; there was a piano at school and she could play music, not just tunes.

'Good,' one of the examiners said when she had finished. He was a large, fleshy man, well-greased; he looked like a prosperous butcher. 'And now we would like you to sing for us.' He handed her another sheet of music.

'I don't feel like singing,' Miriam Lewis had said, and in the silence that followed, 'I will not sing a note.' Who did they think they were, sitting there like three monkeys.

'Can't you sing?' a second man asked in a high, nervous voice. He looked like a draper, the sort who sold women's ready-made underclothes and simpered over them. 'You played the piano so nicely.'

'I don't feel like singing.' Of course she could sing. Who did they think she was, she'd taught singing for three years. Simply, she wouldn't lower herself to humour them.

'We'll have the next young lady, please,' the third man told the usher who was standing at the door, jumpy as a rabbit. 'That will be all, Miss Lewis.' The third examiner was a decent-looking man; she'd felt a little sorry not to have been able to oblige him.

And that was it.

She'd suffered a great deal in the following months, wondering how she was going to explain her failure to her mother and Mr Jenkins. It had cost five pounds to sit the examination, another two for the train fare to Swansea and the accommodation, no one got their certificate without satisfying the examiners in every subject. She finally got her results. She had passed with a distinction in every subject, including music.

She had told Mr Jenkins, then, about her refusal to sing for the gentlemen fools.

'Yes, I heard about that,' he said. Perhaps someone had written to him, he wouldn't elaborate, but gave it as his opinion that what he called her 'donkey streak' could only be an asset to her in the teaching profession.

She remembered – a little ruefully – what he had said, as she watched Josi Evans ride away.

Josi rode home almost enjoying his humiliation at the hands of the little schoolmistress.

'Who does she think she is?' Nano demanded, when he told her what had happened.

'She thinks she's as good as anyone else,' Josi said, 'and she's quite right.'

'Huh!'

In due course, Catrin got first prize in the junior solo and Josi was so pleased that he bought her a new pony which they called Melody.

He didn't see Miss Lewis again for some months, though he thought about her grave, unsmiling face from time to time.

In July that year, Tom came home from school with measles. He was feverish for several days, having to lie in a darkened bedroom when he wanted to be out fishing and roaming the woods. One evening, when he was convalescing, but as usual bemoaning his luck, Doctor Andrews, there on his daily visit, grew impatient and told him how fortunate he was to be getting better so soon. The Rhydfelen schoolmistress almost died of the measles,' he told him. 'She had to stay in bed six weeks; she's still not back at school.'

'I hadn't heard about Miss Lewis's illness,' Josi told the doctor as he took him downstairs. 'Where does she live? I'll send her some of our peaches.'

And the next day he gathered the choicest of the hothouse peaches, arranged them in a basket with a frill of leaves, and took them himself to Rhydfelen. It seemed a strange attention to pay to someone who had done nothing but refuse him a small favour, but Josi was a strange man.

Miriam Lewis was in the garden of her cottage when Josi rode up. She was sitting in a basket-chair, a shawl over her shoulders and another over her knees. He left his horse at the gate and strode up the path, but as he reached her, found himself afflicted by a most unusual shyness.

'Doctor Andrews told us you'd been ill,' he said.

Without another word, he deposited the basket at her feet.

Miss Lewis was as tongue-tied as he.

An elderly woman came out of the cottage.

'My auntie,' Miss Lewis said. 'Hetty Lewis. Auntie, this is Mr Evans, Hendre Ddu.'

Auntie proved as voluble as the other two were silent.

'Oh, there's lovely peaches and how kind of you, Mr Evans. Miriam, well, she's had such kindness from everyone. She's only been here since September, but the people, oh, they've taken her to their hearts and no mistake. Strawberries she's had and runner beans already, and only July. Eleven chickens altogether. You can't die now, I told her, you can't expect wreaths on top of all these chickens. It would be selfish, wouldn't it, Mr Evans? No, the Good Lord has spared her as Mr Jones, Soar, said this morning, to carry on her good work in Rhydfelen. And now she'll have to go to chapel a bit more, won't she, that's what I say.'

'Perhaps Mr Evans would like a cup of tea,' Miss Lewis suggested. Josi's eyes hadn't left her face during her aunt's recital.

'I would,' Josi said.

'Fetch yourself a chair,' Miriam said. 'Go in through the back door and you're in the kitchen.'

'Better for you both to come to the parlour, it's getting quite cool now.'

Miriam stood up obediently, but before she had been able to adjust her shawls, Josi had picked her up and carried her through the kitchen and into the little dark parlour. She was as light as a child.

'Are we friends, then?' Josi asked, while they were alone.

She didn't answer but both were aware of what was hovering over them.

Josi drank his cup of tea and left.

At this time, Miriam Lewis was courting. Her sweetheart was a bank clerk from Henblas who used to cycle to Rhydfelen every Sunday afternoon to have tea with her. His name was Gareth Vaughan, and he was hard-working, religious, and bound, people said, to get on. His father, working at the same bank, had got on, so that he was under-manager when he died, and had left his widow with a house and a good annuity.

In a way, Miriam would have liked to marry Gareth; he was gentle and considerate. He was fairly intelligent, or at least not stupid. She even liked his mother.

He spoke of selling his mother's terraced house in the old part of the town and buying one of the new villas being built on the Carmarthen Road. His mother liked the idea; they were double-fronted, detached houses, and she would be perfectly happy, she said, with a sitting room of her own, and the front garden to potter about in.

Gareth had said they could have a piano and that Miriam could give lessons. They would have a little maid. There was a sizeable garden at the back, he would grow vegetables there; in a few years would be able to afford a greenhouse.

Miriam was never anything but non-committal, she'd think about it, that was the most she'd say. Yet one day she had gone, alone, to the building site and tried to imagine what married life would be like. One or two of the houses were almost completed; solid, square, red-bricked, with square bay windows on the ground floor. Gareth had mentioned the large, airy kitchen with tiled floor and modern range; the scullery behind.

She tried to imagine choosing furniture and curtains, but couldn't. She tried to imagine herself cleaning and shopping and preparing meals for Gareth, but couldn't. The unfinished house she was looking at made her feel nervous and inadequate.

As Miriam Lewis, schoolmistress, she had duties and obligations which she didn't shirk, but they were a result of what she was, and had chosen to become. She felt unfitted, completely unfitted, to undertake Mrs Gareth Vaughan's burdens. Having to conform, doing what the neighbours did, going to chapel on Sunday; being not only a wife, a daughter-in-law, probably a mother, but a member of a respectable, red-bricked society.

'I can't marry you, Gareth,' she had told him, the next time he'd cycled over to see her.

'You may change your mind,' he'd said. Which was what he always said.

One Sunday afternoon shortly afterwards, she had had a surprise visit from Ifan Jenkins her old schoolmaster, and his wife; Mrs Jenkins, it turned out, had relatives living nearby. They met Gareth Vaughan, though very briefly, because he was on the point of cycling home to the evening service at Henblas.

'Who'd have believed it,' Lisi Jenkins had said after he had gone. 'Such an eligible young man.'

'How can you tell how eligible he is?' old Jenkins had asked sourly, 'and you only clapped eyes on him for five minutes.'

'Such a lovely suit and such good manners. And when I think what a little...' Lisi Jenkins halted. She was a tactless woman, not very bright, and Ifan was getting more hot-tempered than ever in old age.

'Go on,' said Miriam, always amused by Lisi's indiscretions.

'A poor little thing you were, indeed, no more flesh on your bones than a gipsy child. Hair cut off because of the nits. Dressed in shreds and patches. Never mind. People can rise these days, and that's not such a bad thing, surely. The lady's maid in Gwynant married Mr Edmund, and her ladyship visits her, they say, though Gladys Pugh who told me isn't the world's most reliable....'

Ifan Jenkins got to his feet as though to rise above his wife's chatter.

'Are you marrying this man, then?' he asked.

'I'm considering it,' Miriam said.

'If you have to consider it, don't,' Jenkins said, 'that's my opinion.'

'I'm all right as I am,' Miriam agreed.

'I should think you are. As right as anyone can be. Your own boss, very near. Someone will come along, no doubt, and you'll marry him because you can't help yourself, but until that time comes, rejoice in your freedom; that's my advice.'

'I think perhaps you're right.'

'Have you ever known me wrong?'

'I'm not going to marry you, Gareth,' she had told him again, the following Sunday. He went on coming to see her, though, went on proposing from time to time, but without much hope. He was not what she wanted; they both knew it.

When Josi came into her life, she realized that he was the someone Ifan Jenkins had warned her about, the one against whom she would have no defences. But he was already married, so what was the good of that?

SEVEN

The married man rode past Miriam's garden often that summer. He and she would usually talk together for a short time under the rowan trees that overhung the path, but he was never again invited into the house; there seemed no excuse for it. I'm a respectable schoolmistress, Miriam told herself. I'm not for him.

The affair languished during autumn and winter, she saw him once at a Christmas concert; a curt nod, that was all.

Gareth continued faithful, and though he made no headway with her, seemed fairly contented.

Miriam put heart and soul into her work. The Inspector of Schools gave her a glowing report. 'The mistress, Miss Miriam Lewis, is a young woman of rare perception and application. Her pupils have responded well to her love of the written word, displaying a mature knowledge of both English and Welsh literature. Arithmetic is taught systematically and thoroughly, the pupils having a commendable grasp of the processes they employ. In Nature Study and Art, a particular measure of excellence has been achieved by the method of taking the children out of doors whenever possible, enabling them to see the wonders surrounding them. They sing harmoniously and joyfully. I have no hesitation in stating that the pupils of Rhydfelen School are being educated in the fullest sense of the word.'

Miriam was gratified by the report, fairly satisfied with the way her life was going.

Yet, when she caught a glimpse of Josi in Llanfryn one Saturday morning in early spring, she waved and rushed to catch up with him; was at his side before she realized what she had done.

I'll ride over to see you one of these days,' he said, confidence in his voice, entreaty in his dark eyes. He didn't understand her, had been trying to put her out of his mind.

They stood together for a minute or more, and in that time, each accepted his fate. Neither of them smiled. The sun shone in the pale sky above them. It was a cold day, glittering like a jewel.

The following Monday, he rode up to the school as he had done almost exactly a year before. Once again he waited outside for all the children to leave.

When he went in, Miriam was at her desk writing. She didn't seem surprised to see him, perhaps she had heard his horse, perhaps she had been expecting him for the past year.

He stood against the door looking at her. Neither of them spoke.

The distance between them. Neither of them moved. Why doesn't she say something, Josi asked himself, why doesn't she help me, why doesn't she smile? The distance between them seemed like distance in a dream.

Then at last Miriam put down her pen, wiping the nib carefully, and Josi took a deep breath and bridged the distance between them, arrived at her side and drew her to her feet. He felt as though he had swum through a river to save a drowning man; that he was the drowning man. For several moments he held her, held on to her. Then he took off his top-coat and spread it on the floor by the little stove and they lay down together.

'Someone will come,' Miriam said.

'I locked the door.'

They lay together in the cold schoolroom until it was quite dark, until, through the narrow windows, built high in the walls to prevent the children catching sight of the lovely world outside, they could see the first white stars.

'I came to this school when I was a boy.'

'I know. I found your name in an old register. Joshua Matthew Evans.'

'You look for my name then, do you?'

'No. You were on the list when the school opened. I noticed it.'

'You happened to notice it?' Josi's voice had a laugh in it and a hint of danger, too. She was aware of both.

'Why is that? Because you love me? You do love me, don't you? I know you do.'

'I saw your photograph, too, in the first log book. About twelve,

60

I think. Such a great, scowling boy. Joshua Matthew Evans.'

'Have you ever been in love before, Miriam?'

'Not before, not now either.'

The moon rose and the sky lightened.

'I must go home. They'll be out looking for me.'

'Who will?'

'Someone. Neli Morris, Nant Eithin, will notice there's no light.'

'You shall go home when you've told me you love me.'

'Is that important? After what's happened?'

'It's more important after what's happened. I know you love me. Say it, Miriam.'

'I don't love anyone else, that's all I can say.'

'You mustn't see that bank clerk any more, that's one thing. It's not fair on him.'

'I shall decide that. In my own good time.'

There was silence between them again for a minute or two. An owl hooted in the clear, frosty night.

'Oh Miriam, it isn't fair on me,' Josi said at last. 'I love you, Miriam. You mustn't see him again, you mustn't. I love you. I can't bear it. Come, I'll take you home.'

'I love you,' he said again when they reached the cottage. As they kissed, Miriam could feel the tears on his face. She tried to see his face in the dark.

Josi adored her; her lively mind, her toughness, her complete acceptance of the situation which he found so difficult to accept.

'This isn't the life for you,' he would say as he held her in his arms on the classroom floor, on the hillside bracken in summer, eventually in her little cottage, in spite of the danger of it.

'You gave me enough time to think it over,' she would say, 'I'd decided to have you long before you'd come round to it.'

'Oh, it's me they'll all blame,' she would say. 'The shameless hussy. Lusting after his body and her only a little bit of a thing, wouldn't you think she could have been satisfied with less, Gareth Vaughan's, say.'

To Josi with his strict chapel upbringing, to hear a girl talking openly and delightedly about the joys of sex, using a fair sprinkling of the words he'd been thrashed for knowing as a boy, went to his head. He would never have enough of her, he knew it. She was as important to him as the weather.

Every time he went to the cottage – late, so as to avoid any likelihood of other callers – it was like the first time; his heart racing. When they met by accident, in a concert or singing festival or public meeting, he would address only a few words to her, but his eyes would return to her for the rest of the evening. If another man talked to her or hung about her, he was tormented; not with jealousy; he knew now that she loved him; but because he, himself, was not able to be at her side.

However careful they might be in public, there were the few occasions when someone saw them together and naturally there was a certain amount of talk. Once, they had bumped into Lowri, at that time the second maid at Hendre Ddu. She lived in a hillside hamlet about a mile outside Rhydfelen, and Josi, having forgotten that it was her day off, was taking Miriam for an evening walk that way. When they met, Lowri had blushed and Miriam, on his arm, had grown pale. Josi had made some remark about a lily and a rose and tried to laugh. It was weeks after that before Lowri could look at him without blushing; Josi felt sorry and a little ashamed at the extent of her embarrassment. Somehow, though, he knew that she would never breathe a word about the encounter and he was right; she was a good girl.

In fact no one was malicious enough to let Rachel hear even a whisper of the affair. Josi was a popular figure, a hero to many; the poor boy who had got himself the best farm in the district, how could he be expected to behave like anyone else? Had they heard that he was compromising Lady Harris's elegant daughter, the Honourable Priscilla, it would have surprised no one; the fact that he had chosen such an ordinary, homespun girl, hardly pretty, let alone beautiful, seemed to display a most commendable modesty. 'Good old Josi,' they said.

'Good old Josi. He rides over to see the little schoolmistress now and again. Well, nobody's too old for a bit of extra schooling. One and one makes three, that will be the end of it, though, mark my words.'

They were proved right.

When Josi discovered that Miriam was pregnant he felt utterly happy; liberated from the bonds which had kept him tied to Rachel for so long. He was still conscious of his sin – he believed implicitly in the ten commandments – but as a sinner he could now allow that his clearest duty lay with Miriam.

Miriam was not much concerned with sin or the ten commandments. Although as a teacher she had to pay it lip service, she had rejected the religion of her youth and could see no reason to search for another. She acknowledged the beauty of psalms and gospels, but didn't care to be comforted by empty words; she had seen 'God is Love' displayed in homes filled with hate, 'God shall provide' above bare boards, while the most popular text, 'Death is profit', seemed a shameful denial of the value and beauty of life.

She had no desire either to feel washed from sin or immortal. She acknowledged that there were many 'saints' whose enlightenment in the dark ages of superstition and cruelty had shone forth before men, but believed their vision to be a manifestation of their humanity rather than their divinity. As for herself, she was a most imperfect human being, she knew it, and could not do without Josi. And the price she had to pay was the knowledge that she was harming Rachel, when her most ardent wish was to harm no one; man, child nor beast.

She had to have Josi. Sometimes she dreamed that she had given him up and woke up sweating and trembling.

Miriam's attitude to her pregnancy altered from day to day, almost from hour to hour. She was sad that she would have to give up teaching which she enjoyed, and leave the cottage which had been her home for six years; the only comfortable home she had ever had. She knew that she would also have to leave the village where she had been happy – even if she had been able to get lodgings there and been capable of holding up her head as an unmarried mother, her presence would affect Josi's standing in the community; to be reputedly engaged in an affair was one thing, having a mistress and child quite another – she knew she had to leave.

But while she would be struggling with the problem of where to go, how long her savings would last, how to bring up an illegitimate child, happiness would break in like a shaft of sunlight; Josi's child and hers was there deep inside her, the act made flesh, she wasn't barren as she had often thought: the miracle of procreation filled her.

She remembered – she was quite a small child at the time – her mother taking hold of one of her hands and putting an egg into it, a large white egg. She had felt the mysterious pulsing inside the thin, smooth warmth of the shell. 'That's the chick,' her mother had said, replacing the egg under the hen. The wonder of that moment had remained with Miriam through a quarter of a century.

She gave in her notice before the Christmas holidays. She told everyone she was leaving because she had to return to her family. Many, though, while pretending to believe her, formed other conjectures which were nearer the truth.

The deputy director of education came to the school a week before she left at the end of February, and after thanking her for her years of loyal service, looked her full in the face and asked her whether there was a chance of her getting married. 'There's no chance of it,' she said.

He shook hands with her sadly.

'You'll all remember Miss Lewis,' he told the children. 'No need for me to say anything. You'll all remember her. For what we have received may the Lord make us truly thankful, isn't it.'

She had asked that there should be no farewell party. Two heavy brass candlesticks were presented to her, though, on the last day; a former pupil had made a door-to-door collection and found a ready response. The children brought her snowdrops and catkins and birds' eggs. By the end of the day, most of the girls were in tears; one of the big boys cried too, though he said it was because a piece of chalk had got stuck in his nose.

She moved to Llanfryn where her aunt, her father's only surviving sister, lived in a small terraced house. After three or four months of sickness and anxiety it seemed the only place she could go to, she hadn't the energy or the spirit to make any other arrangements.

Hetty Lewis, who had nursed her willingly and cheerfully enough through the attack of measles six years earlier, was almost eighty by this time and didn't take kindly to the irregularity of the situation. 'It isn't right for you to go to strangers, I suppose,' she'd said. 'All the same, I can't say that you're welcome. No, I don't like it a bit, not a bit.'

Though she had not been capable of turning her niece away, she often refused to talk to her for days at a time. She wouldn't let her go out except late at night, and made her rush upstairs if anyone came to call. 'This is a respectable house, this is,' she would say, if Miriam dared to grumble at the way she was treated.

And when Josi came to her door, bold as brass and determined to see Miriam, it seemed the last straw. 'This isn't right, Mr Evans, no indeed. What will my neighbours think.' He had almost to force his way into the house. She wouldn't allow him to be on his own with Miriam however much he would argue that it was bolting the stable door too late. 'This is my house, this is, and I won't have any goings-on. There's been too many goings-on between you and my niece if you ask me, and a pretty pass it's brought her to and what can you do about it? Nothing.'

She never believed that Josi intended to leave Hendre Ddu when his son returned from Oxford for the summer, indeed would have thought no more of him if she had, marriage being sacrosanct in her eyes.

Every Sunday, morning and evening, after she had been to chapel she would insist on going over the sermon so that Miriam should not be entirely cut off from the chance of salvation. She would often stray from the kindly precepts of her present minister to the sterner teachings of her earliest mentors, their insistence on the flaming tortures of hell. And finally, realizing that Miriam didn't show the right degree of concern about the wailing and gnashing of teeth, almost every sermon she relayed would contain reference to David's adulterous love for Bathsheba and God's punishment in the death of their son.

This always roused Miriam. Hadn't Christ come to teach a different morality? she would ask. Hadn't he said that hypocrisy was the worst sin? Hadn't he forgiven the prostitute and the woman taken in adultery?

At which Hetty, bewildered and angry at Miriam's daring to cross such thorny ground, would point to her and shout, 'Go thou and sin no more.' And Miriam, in spite of her fury would be left shaken and close to tears. It was a miserable time.

Only when the baby was almost due did Hetty relent a little and suggest that Miriam should go out for a bit of a walk.

'You'd better see the midwife while you're out. She'll be needed before too long if I'm any judge. Mrs Howells, 3 Cothi Crescent. She'll tell the whole town, but what can we do.'

It was a May afternoon, sunny, after a morning of rain. Miriam had to walk to the outskirts of the town – a distance of about half a mile. Her freedom after long confinement dazed her, the air was so aqueous it seemed to swirl round her, leaves had never been so green, blackbirds had never sung so riotously. But it was the smell of the lilac that she remembered afterwards whenever she thought of that afternoon. Impossible to describe, the clean, fresh beauty of it; its hint of sorrow. Lilies of the valley were for a first love, too sickly sweet, even the old moss roses in the garden at home, which her mother called Mary's roses, not after the virgin, but after the friend who had given her the cuttings, even the old roses had a cloying quality, you smelled them and it was suddenly too much. But not lilac. You could smell it for ever. She broke off a branch and took great breaths of its scent and walked on as though drugged.

She must have walked for well over an hour. Without realizing it, she was just outside Rhydfelen, had covered a distance of almost five miles. And there was nothing for it but to retrace her steps. She dared not call anywhere to ask for a cup of tea, dared not even rest in the high cow parsley at the roadside in case someone passed and noticed her condition.

She had walked back only a short way when Doctor Andrews overtook her in his car. He had almost to carry her to the passenger seat.

She gave him her aunt's address and he drove her there and remained with her to deliver her premature baby.

'Is there anyone I can contact for you, Miss Lewis?' he asked her before he left. 'In my profession I've learnt to be as silent as the hills.'

But Miriam would only smile and say nothing. She suspected that he already knew her secret. She held her little girl in her arms, marvelling at her. She looked so like Josi; how could the doctor fail to know whose baby she was. She lay back on her pillow and the afternoon air seemed to be lapping round her still; like ribbons of water.

Doctor Andrews left, promising to contact the midwife before he went home.

Hetty came in then, and cried over her great-niece and kissed Miriam for the first time since she had arrived. And the next evening when Josi came, she tip-toed out of the room and left them together.

EIGHT

His father was already at The Sheaf when Tom arrived there on Saturday night.

He had resolved not to begin with recriminations; he intended to talk calmly and reasonably about his decision to leave Oxford, the possibility of Catrin's going to Art School, the day-to-day running of the farm. All the same, when he caught sight of his father and went to join him at the corner table of the lounge bar, his composure quite deserted him. 'You've left us, then,' he said.

Josi was intolerably moved by Tom's voice and expression. He pushed a mug of beer towards him. 'None of that nonsense. We're father and son, aren't we. Nothing can alter that. Drink up now.'

Tom raised his tankard and almost emptied it in one smooth swallow.

'Oh, steady on,' his father said. Due to his strict Methodist upbringing, Josi's drinking was usually restricted to a moderate half-pint on market days. 'If your grandfather could see you, my boy, he'd turn in his grave.'

'Teetotaller, was he? The old man?'

The danger was over; they both felt it.

'A hundred per cent. A miser too.'

'And a criminal, according to you.'

'No, no, that was his father, Thomas, the one you're named after, he was the crook. Old Thomas Morgan, Hendre Ddu, was the one that smiled and spoke fair and cheated and robbed and throve like the green bay tree. You know what he'd do, don't you. I've told you before, he'd lend some poor little dabs a hundred pounds when the harvest was bad; no interest, only a little clause in the contract that if they couldn't pay it back by such-and-such – and it seemed such a long way ahead – he'd have their bit of a farm instead. Done. Signed. Wait. Grab. Esger Gog. Ffynnon Fair, Garth Lwyd, Ffos-y-ffin. Do you know how I know? My grandfather, Amos Evans, Cefn Hebog, was one of the fools, see, that signed away his little inheritance. A small farm it was, less than twenty acres, but it had been in the family for close on four centuries, what's that, about sixteen generations. I've got reason to know, I have.'

'You should have steered clear of the Morgans, then, shouldn't you? Touch pitch and be defiled.'

'Aye, I should have steered clear of them, indeed I should. But if I had, you wouldn't be here for a start, and I'm glad you are, somehow, drunkard or not. Anyway, old Thomas Morgan wasn't all bad, I don't say that. He did a lot for the area one way or another. For instance he gave three acres of good land in the middle of Henblas for a cemetery, so that the people he squeezed to death could have a decent burial in the dry. He probably did something quite substantial for the workhouse in Llanfryn too. I don't want you to think he was all bad.'

'We're imperfect, all of us,' Tom said, significantly.

'Yes indeed. We are indeed. Though your mother is less imperfect than most of us, I admit it. She was sent away to a Christian school and taught to be charitable and virtuous to atone for the sins of her fathers and she is a good woman, I mean it, but difficult to live up to. She's kind and gracious and quickly moved to pity and once she had something more but that dried up years ago. But she's a good woman, I've said so, and I hope you'll never let her down as I have.'

'I hope not to,' Tom said. A lofty silence settled on them. Tom got his pipe out and Josi sat back in his chair and started to hum. He looked about him and nodded at various people.

'Is it a boy or a girl?' Tom asked. At last.

'A girl,' Josi said. He sighed as he thought of her. A little creature she was, not much bigger than a leveret, but she'd caused a good deal of trouble one way or another. Mari-Elen they'd called her, after his mother and Miriam's, two women who'd died young from poverty and over-work. 'Hard work never killed anyone is the greatest lie since God shall provide.' He could hear Miriam's voice in his head. If Miriam died, his life would be over. Even thinking about it made him feel cold. He took a draught of beer and saw that Tom was still looking at him.

'A girl,' he said again. 'Boys are too much trouble altogether; they go their own ways and they drink like fish. A girl. So big.' He held his large hands out in front of him, about a foot apart. 'She looks a cross little thing at the moment, not unlike you round the eyes.'

Tom felt a heaviness in his chest, as though he'd swallowed a stone with his beer. He remembered having the same sort of feeling as a boy, whenever his father had cuffed him; the pain of the blow had been nothing.

'I hear you're going away,' he said.

'That's right. It's best, isn't it, all in all. I've been offered the job I went for and it's as good as I'll get. Llwyn Cadno Farm, South Cardiganshire. The owner of the place, Isaac Lloyd his name is, knows how I'm placed and doesn't seem to mind. I told him straight out and he said "You're a bloody fool, then, but it's none of my business. I want an experienced man, so your loss is my gain." Thinking about it since, I've wondered if that's why he offered me such a poor wage; because he knew I couldn't turn it down. Imperfect beings all of us. Never mind. I dare say we'll survive, won't we, all of us, what do you say?'

'About that twenty pounds, Dad, you can forget about that.'

'Did your mother tell you to say that?'

'I'm saying it.'

'No, no, I'll pay it back. If she'd said it, it would be different.'

'She hasn't said anything, one way or another.'

'I'll wait till she does then, and abide with that.'

Josi refused another drink and left within the hour.

As soon as he'd gone, Tom realized that they hadn't talked of any of the things he'd had on his mind, he was no wiser even about what clothes his father wanted, all he knew was the name of the farm he was going to.

His father had left without any ceremony, as though he'd be seeing him again later that night. There was little ceremony about his father; no fuss, no show. He suddenly saw him resting at the side of a hedge, his whole body completely relaxed so that he seemed almost a part of the landscape. He seemed extraordinarily at peace with himself; even at the present time, with his life completely disrupted, that was the impression he gave. Whereas he, Tom, felt an alien wherever he was, both in Oxford and back in Wales. He called for his third pint of beer. What could alter his life, he wondered, give him a sense of purpose, a place in the world?

Love? Religion? Neither seemed to have the power to move him. He dreaded the empty Sunday ahead. He'd go to chapel, of course. He probably didn't get more out of it than Catrin did, but it didn't seem worth making a fuss about; grieving his mother. If only Edward was still with them. He could talk to Edward. Even about his father.

Josi walked quickly towards Hetty Lewis's house in Cambrian Street. It was the first time he'd ever lived in a town, and though it was a small one, surrounded on all sides by hills and fields, he felt hemmed in. In three days, he and Miriam were leaving for the farm on the other side of the mountain; it would be a hard life, but not impossible like living in the middle of bricks and chimney pots.

Hetty had already had her bowl of gruel and gone to bed and Miriam was suckling the baby in front of the fire.

The best kitchen was small and cosy as a burrow. Josi sat in the large fireside chair, an old chair of elm and oak, shaped and polished by years of human contact like the handle of his scythe. He ran his hands along the curved arms; feeling the proximity of others comforted him always.

He and Miriam didn't speak; the baby was easily distracted, interested in everything except feeding. When at last she would take no more, Josi took her from Miriam.

Her dark plum-coloured eyes were wide open but unseeing; she seemed knocked out by milk. 'Elen,' he said. She tried to focus on him, but yawned instead; a brief, pink yawn. Afterwards she resumed her blind gazing.

He handed her back to Miriam.

'Won't she do for you?'

'She's all right. She's all right.'

'She's filling out. Even Auntie Hetty says so.'

'She's all right. She's all right. It's just that she won't have much of a life, that's all.'

'You mean, because she's a hedge child.'

'That's a very coarse expression.'

'I don't know any other, That's what she is, anyway. In fact, she's more of a hedge child than most. She was born in a hedge as well, very near.'

'I wasn't thinking of that, anyway. I was only thinking of her being brought up poor. It's no joke.'

'You and I survived. She'll survive too. She looks a little fighter. Look at her fists. Anyway, I can think of plenty of people worse off than us, we'll have ten shillings a week and a cottage.'

'A pretty poor cottage with nothing decent to go in it.'

'Are you regretting Hendre Ddu already?'

'Of course not. I never cared for Hendre Ddu.'

Miriam didn't reply but looked at him sadly. That was her greatest worry; that he had made an over-hasty decision.

'It wasn't the farm I ever wanted, it was Rachel. Does that make it worse? It wasn't that I was so much in love with her, only triumphant, somehow, that she was so much in love with me. Can you understand that? She was older than I was, a large gracious woman who looked as though she'd never been young and yet she was as silly about me as a sixteen-year-old about her first sweetheart; had to have me with her every minute. Her father was deadset against me of course, and I was excited by that, and by the way I won every round. When her father shouted about the damned cheek I'd had, asking her to marry me, I said I never had, she had asked me. It was the truth but I shouldn't have said so, I know. Only I hated him; everybody did. When he died there wasn't so much in it for me. And when she'd had Tom and Catrin; she had a bad time with Catrin, I'll give her that; she thought the farm would be enough for me. But it wasn't, it never was. I could never be interested in grappling and grasping for more and more profit. That's how people get rich, by loving money, thinking of nothing else, becoming slaves to it. Old Griffydd Morgan used to wait for his ha'penny change. He'd insist on his discounts, even from little traders almost going bankrupt. When he bought, he could afford to wait till prices were low, but he never sold low. Nobody ever had a bargain from him. I don't get pleasure from doing people down. Having a bit of money is fine, of course it is, but if it's in your blood to make it grow and grow, it's the devil taking over, that's how it seems to me. Anyway, it was never my farm but Rachel's so I saved my soul. I'm not saying I wouldn't like to be able to buy a little place, I would, but I wouldn't get rich. I'd work hard. I can't help that, it's in my nature to work hard, but I know when to stop and I know how to enjoy other things. You know that.'

For the first time, the way he was looking at her made Miriam sad. 'You've had other women,' she said.

'No one.' Josi thought it was true. The others hadn't counted. 'No one but you. Whatever made you say that? Miriam, what's the matter?'

She had turned from him and was looking into the dying fire.

'I saw your daughter in Llanfryn on Thursday morning. She was in Lloyd the Chemist's.'

'Catrin? Why didn't you tell me? What happened?'

'She followed me into the street. She just wanted me to know, she said, that you'd had plenty of other women before me and would have plenty after.'

Josi said nothing for several moments. After a time he got up from his chair and came to sit at Miriam's knees and kissed her hand. 'Only you and I know,' he said. 'Only us two. Oh, I'm sorry about Catrin. I'm sorry about everything. We both knew how it would be for you, didn't we? At least I'm with you now. We can't get married, but we're together. Aren't we? We're together.'

'I've got a few things in Rhydfelen,' Miriam said in quite a different voice – her schoolteacher voice which he hadn't heard for months. 'I left them in Nant Eithin's barn. Neli Morris said she'd mind them for me till I sent for them. We should take them with us when we go; it'll cost more to send for them later. They're only odds and ends but they'll be useful, blankets and so on, pots and pans, two chairs and a chest of drawers that belonged to my mother.'

'I'll fetch them on Monday. I'll borrow a cart from someone.'

'Won't you be afraid of people talking?'

'They've talked enough by this time. Why should I mind? Do you think I'm ashamed of you?'

'You should be. And of yourself.'

'You're not ashamed.'

'I'm not religious like you are, so I don't feel the same. I feel sorrowful about your family, even Catrin. I don't like to think of your wife who's a good, kind woman, everyone says so, whom I've wronged. But the wrong's done. Neither of us could choose differently so I try not to feel ashamed. Life's hard enough without that. I know you feel bad about moving from this place.'

73

'Not at all. We're only crossing an old mountain. Only thirty miles. Some of my people went to America when times were bad, we're only moving to another county.'

'A different place, though. Different people.'

'Poorer, that's all. Land's not so fertile, that's all. What does it matter. I like a challenge; a bit of a struggle.'

The baby was fast asleep, her little face old and resigned as though she knew already that life was a struggle, one way or another. Miriam handed her to Josi again while she made the fire safe and got a candle to take them upstairs.

'I hope to God we don't have too many of these,' Josi said. 'They're nice little things, I know, but they all have to be fed and watered.'

NINE

Catrin spent a miserable Saturday.

She had always felt thoroughly at ease with Edward Turncliffe. She had never been wary of him as she was with other young men; he was her brother's friend, and in any case engaged to be married. She had allowed herself to think of him as a friend, one of her few friends, so that the new feelings he had aroused in her filled her with shame and anger; a new and deeper relationship was the last thing she had wanted.

The idea of marriage had always been so abhorrent to her. She hated weddings – she seemed to go to so many – merriment for everyone except the poor bride who generally looked timid and embarrassed. And if the broadest of the jokes were anything to go by, the wedding breakfast was only a preliminary to a farm-yard kind of coupling, leading as inevitably to the first pregnancy; the bride of a few months by this time pale and big-bellied, the finery of the wedding and the presents forgotten.

Catrin couldn't bear to think that she had nothing to hope from life but the early 'good' marriage which everyone seemed to predict for her. At least she was determined to go to London first. Since her holiday there with Tom the previous year, it had been the focus of all her dreaming; so full of colour and life; art galleries, shops and concerts. If she could spend, say, seven years in London, she was sure that she would be willing to come back then to face the inevitable farmer bridegroom. To her mind, a bride of twenty-five, a mature woman of the world, wasn't a figure of pathos like the innocent bride of eighteen.

She wanted to 'live' first. If she had been asked what exactly she meant by 'living', she wouldn't be certain, she only saw herself moving among beautiful intelligent people, accepted and admired.

She had been in a state of rebellious waiting for over two years. She remembered when it had begun, in the spring following her sixteenth birthday. Before then, she had enjoyed school and certain aspects of her life on the farm, particularly riding; since that time, all her most deeply felt experiences had come from books, she had hardly lived at all at first hand. She had sold her outgrown pony and declined the offer of a horse, her schoolwork began to pall, she found the girls silly and the boys dull and immature.

It was a theological student, preaching at their chapel one Sunday morning, who had brought about the abrupt change from schoolgirl to woman, though it would probably have been someone or something else if not he.

He had been a painfully shy, incoherent preacher, even her mother had seemed a little embarrassed by him and everyone else in the congregation quite openly restless. 'Poor young man,' Miss Rees had said after the benediction. 'His spirit was soaring, I'm sure, but the old words just wouldn't come out.'

They had stayed behind in the little cold chapel to invite him back to dinner. He was grateful indeed, he assured them, but he had made other arrangements. He had shaken hands with them. To her mother and Miss Rees he had stammered out a few conventional words of thanks. Then he had taken Catrin's hand and in very distinct, ringing tones had said, 'I am the Rose of Sharon.'

'Thank you,' Catrin had said, taking her hand away as quickly as she could. She had never seen the strange youth before or since.

Back in the brougham afterwards, her mother had ventured an explanation for the young man's outburst. 'He was trying to tell Catrin that her beauty is a gift from God,' she said. Miss Rees had been glad to agree, she had been a little worried about him, wondering whether the ordeal of preaching the word had gone to his head. Before they had arrived home the two women were firmly agreed that his words were certainly in order and possibly of divine inspiration. 'If he had said "*You* are the rose of Sharon", it would be different,' her mother had said, 'and a little impertinent, but he kept to the scriptures unaltered.'

Her father, told of the incident over beef and Yorkshire pudding, was quite ready to agree with his wife. 'He was still in the high places,' Josi had said. 'No insult intended, I'm sure of it.'

No one was surprised that he should have been struck by her beauty, only that he had commented publicly about it.

Until that Sunday, Catrin had never seriously considered her looks. That afternoon she went to stand in front of the long mirror in her mother's bedroom and studied herself from all angles and accepted her beauty. Nothing had been the same afterwards.

She accepted that she was different.

There had always been a gulf between her and her colleagues at school; now she understood it. Pretty girls generally had a good time at school, they were popular with other girls and teased by the boys and the masters, but beauty obviously set one apart; both boys and girls were rather in awe of it; it was as though the possessor belonged to a slightly different species.

Lowri, one of the maids at Hendre Ddu, seemed to be her only close friend.

It was she, a few months later, who showed her the picture-postcards, a series called Edwardian Beauties which her mother had collected some years earlier. 'This one looks just like you,' Lowri had said. 'I wish you had a dress like that. I wish you'd let me put your hair up.'

And so, on a wet Saturday afternoon, Catrin had borrowed one of her mother's dresses, a pale blue silk she had worn on her honeymoon, and a fan and a shawl, and Lowri had brushed and combed her hair, arranging it in elaborate coils which she piled one on top of the other like fruit in a bowl. Then Catrin had stood with a hand on her hip whilst Lowri had surveyed her. 'Miss Lily Langtry,' she had said. For a time the two girls had giggled together quite happily.

Then Catrin had stepped out of the borrowed dress, letting it fall to the ground in a heap, and pulled out all the hair pins and shaken down her hair and brushed it and plaited it again.

'What's the matter?' Lowri had asked. Catrin looked as though she was about to cry.

'What am I going to do?' she had asked. 'What will become of me?'

Lowri was two years older than Catrin, a good-natured, motherly girl.

'Don't be such a little silly. Nothing is going to become of you, nothing at all. You'll just stay home here with us until you're old enough to get married. And your husband will be very rich and important, a doctor perhaps or a member of parliament, and you'll live in a mansion and have a big motor-car. Now you put your skirt and blouse on quick and come down to the kitchen. Everybody's out and I'll make you a nice cup of tea.'

But Catrin had stayed up in her bedroom crying. She was beautiful, she'd be a fool not to know it, she was different. She wasn't going to stay at home until some idiot would notice her and ask her to marry him. She was going to use her beauty. She wanted....

She wasn't sure what she wanted but she was quite certain that it wasn't marriage and a quiet life in the country.

She had always been impatient by nature. As a small child every fine summer day had agitated her, she had insisted on getting up at the first light and going out with the men, even though she had very soon to return to the house to get ready, after breakfast, for a long walk to school. Miss Rees, worried that such a little creature would over-tire herself, used to coax her to stay in with her, even offering to let her wash the kitchen floor, at that time her special treat; but it was no use, Catrin would just point to the iridescent blue outside and run off.

When a picnic had been promised and had to be postponed, not because of a change in the weather which she had no difficulty in accepting, but because visitors had arrived or for some other 'trivial' reason, she would be inconsolable. 'Tomorrow,' her mother would say. 'We'll go tomorrow, I promise you.' 'Today,' Catrin would shout, stamping her feet or throwing herself on the floor. 'Today. Today. Today.'

At sixteen she was still the same. She had made the discovery that she was beautiful and she had no faith in tomorrow. Beauty was as swiftly-passing as a butterfly or a summer day.

She left school in the July of that year. It wasn't considered proper that a girl of rising seventeen should cycle along country roads in the short skirts of the school uniform. Anyway, further studying wasn't thought necessary since girls didn't go to university.

That year, however, a girl from the sixth form had won a scholarship to an art school and gone to London, and Catrin had seized on that as her most likely chance to escape from home; she had a certain talent in drawing and her mother thought it a lady-like occupation. (She had far more talent for music but unfortunately her mother knew a girl – a nice girl – who had gone to Italy to study singing and she had never returned, had possibly married an Italian and become a Roman Catholic.)

She had waited, sketching and painting every afternoon, keeping herself aloof from the life around her, until she was eighteen and felt she could justifiably insist on her parents making a decision about her.

'Wait till Tom comes home,' her mother had said all that year whenever she had broached the subject. 'We'll see what Tom thinks about it.'

She had waited. And before he had arrived, her father had shattered all her chances of leaving home by leaving himself, and she was so full of resentment that she had followed his mistress, the Rhydfelen schoolteacher, out of the chemist's shop at Llanfryn and shouted abuse at her. The memory of the scene tormented her. For the rest of that day she had remained upstairs with her mother, quite stupefied with shame but not knowing what to do to make amends.

She was still in that state the next morning when she had been asked to drive Edward to the station to catch his train.

He had teased her about wanting to leave home and she had lashed out at him, and what happened afterwards would always leave a mark on her for good or ill; she was aware of that from the beginning.

Her first feelings were that she had been betrayed by a friend she had trusted, but towards evening, other more complicated feelings were beginning to take hold of her, chief amongst them a knowledge that she had been stirred beyond anything she could have imagined.

Although Tom had not told his mother that he intended to see his father that evening, she seemed to sense that something was in the air. 'Where has Tom gone?' she asked Catrin and Miss Rees.

Neither of them knew.

Miss Rees always came to sit with Rachel on a Saturday evening; the custom had started partly as a recognition of the housekeeper's close part in the family, partly because Rachel, from the early days of her marriage, had always been left alone on that evening.

It was the only time in the week – except when she went to morning service on a Sunday – that Miss Rees was ever seen without the starched white apron which enveloped her from her double chin to her knees. ('She's black underneath,' Catrin had whispered to Tom on first seeing Nano in the parlour with her mother.) Her best dress was of stiff bombasine with jet beads sewn on the bodice in such serried profusion that it looked like a breast-plate. She had bought the dress thirteen years before, when Rachel's father, old Griffydd Morgan, had died. It always smelt faintly of camphor and peppermints though she hung it out for an airing every Saturday morning when the weather was fine. She wore it every Saturday evening, every Sunday morning, and to five or six funerals a year, nine in '07 when the winter was particularly hard. It would last her lifetime for sure.

'Where has Tom gone?' Rachel asked again.

'Where do young men go on these fine Saturday nights, Mrs Evans? I'm always wanting to know, but they'll never tell me. Young Dan always says he's going home to see his mother, but when I tease him about the Dijon he's stuck in his jacket, he blushes like a girl, and when I see his mother in chapel she says she doesn't see him from one week to the next and why are we working him so hard.'

'Nano, you're not trying to tell me that Tom has got a sweet-heart, are you?'

'I don't know, I'm sure. It wouldn't surprise me to know that there's a young lady somewhere in these parts very anxious to see him again after so long. Six months is a long spell to young people, I do know that.'

'Do you know anything about it, Catrin?'

Catrin, pleased to see her mother showing a flicker of interest in something outside her own suffering, wished she had the imagina-tion to add some fuel to the tiny spark.

'I'm afraid not,' she said. 'Perhaps he has got a girl. I don't know. He doesn't talk to me.'

'It's a pity, isn't it,' Miss Rees said. 'People not talking to people. Now, there are some who say that I talk too much, but what I say is, it's talking that makes us different from the animals, isn't it. We can talk and I think we should and then we'd all be the wiser.'

Miss Rees was silent for a minute while she turned the heel of a sock. She knitted three pairs of long grey socks for each of the men for New Year's Day, from the thick, oily wool she got from the local mill. ('I keep their bellies full and their feet dry, only God can give them sense.') Mrs Evans and Catrin watched her having her way with the heel.

'Now old Dic Pugh was dumb from birth, poor fellow, but he was a wonderful listener, he showed interest and made the right responses – grunts, really, but that sounds disrespectful. I've had many a hearty conversation with Dic, he didn't withhold himself you see, his silence was warm and eloquent. Now Llew Gelly-Deg was a different animal. He had a good speaking voice – a nice baritone in Soar choir, too, but nothing to say and nothing he wanted to hear from one week's end to another. His wife went back to her parents, eventually, sick of his thin silences, whereas Mati Pugh is still going strong in her seventies, cheerful as a kettle. "Make a joyful noise unto the Lord", I remember that was the text Garfield Roberts took in one of the revival meetings he had on the bank above Henblas bridge, and there's singing we had that day, do you remember, Mrs Evans? Seven hours we were there altogether. That was a noise, right enough. Some of the little ones started to shout with the excitement of it all. "Let them be," Garfield Roberts said. "Let them shout, for God's sake." There was no keeping them quiet in chapel after that, but everything is quiet and orderly again now in all the chapels, quiet as the grave. I don't know who said silence is golden but I'm sure it wasn't the Lord, he had more sense.'

Catrin had been telling the truth when she told her mother that Tom never talked to her. That night, though, when he came home from Llanfryn — their mother and Miss Rees had long gone to bed — he did.

She was still sitting at the table; she had undertaken to mend a lace collar for her mother and it was proving a more complicated job than she had expected. He came in and sat opposite her, and when she got up to adjust the light he seemed afraid that she was about to go.

'You're not going to bed, are you?' he said. 'Not yet, surely?'

She looked at him with surprise. Of course he was missing Edward and their father, that would explain his sudden desire for her company. Or that he was the worse – or the better – for drink.

He looked tired and dejected. He's not handsome, Catrin thought, but he's got a strong face, a face that has more character when it's shadowed. When he was a boy, I thought him ugly, his nose was too long; now it's a good nose, a good head; a head I'd like to draw. Thomas Morgan Evans, Hendre Ddu.

'Do you know the people at The Wheatsheaf?' he asked her. 'They came from Swansea. Jack and Elsie Morris. Been at Llanfryn six or seven years. Do you know them?'

Catrin admitted that she didn't.

'No, I didn't think you would. Not the sort of people you'd get to meet, I suppose. Quite a decent little couple. The wife's from Bristol I think. They've only got one child, a daughter, about sixteen, and she's got herself in the family way.'

Catrin made no comment. She wondered what possible reason Tom had for relating such a sordid piece of gossip to her, when only a few nights earlier he had seemed to be reproving her for knowing the facts of life.

'The poor old thing,' he said. To himself, it seemed.

'Won't she get married, then? She'd be quite a catch, wouldn't she? The only daughter of a prosperous pub?'

'No, she's one of these half-witted girls; shapeless, with slightly bulging blue eyes and little plump hands and feet. No one will marry her, that's for sure. She won't even tell them who the father is; she just looks bashful, apparently, when they question her. They didn't notice her condition for months, perhaps she'd forgotten all about the man by the time they did. Let's hope so.'

'Her parents will look after her, though, won't they?'

'I suppose so. Her father kept saying that an illegitimate baby will ruin her chances, but the poor thing never had any chances. Who would take advantage of a girl like that, that's what I'd like to know. Her father thinks it may have been one of the fairground men; I suppose it could have been any of the local louts who'd had too much to drink at the Michaelmas Fair.'

'When is the baby due?'

'No idea. Some time soon. I suppose the baby will be all right. The grandparents will look after it, I suppose. It may be a normal, healthy child.'

'Perhaps the poor thing will be a good mother.'

'She's half-witted, girl. Simple.'

They sat in silence for a while, Catrin at a complete loss for words. Should she get up, she wondered, and light herself a lamp? Wish Tom a brusque good night? It was late, well past her usual bedtime.

But the atmosphere between them seemed charged, somehow, so that she couldn't bring herself to speak or move.

'Do you understand any of it?' Tom asked at last. 'I mean *any* of it. Father, and so on? *Any* of it?'

'No, not really,' Catrin said.

All the same, she knew she was not being absolutely truthful. Since the encounter with Edward the previous morning, one of life's mysteries had been briefly, fitfully, illuminated.

TEN

Josi, Miriam and the baby left Cambrian Street, Llanfryn at five o'clock on the morning of Midsummer Day. Their scant belongings included the bed and table, cupboard, chairs and mangle which had used up most of the money Josi had taken from the bank before leaving Hendre Ddu, and Miriam's few things which he had fetched from Rhydfelen the previous day.

The haulier, old Robin Jones, had done several odd jobs for Josi in the past and had been glad to help him with the move. He seemed to regard Josi and Miriam's setting out together as the most unremarkable thing in the world. 'Not many would want to do this for me, Robin bach,' Josi had said the previous night.

'Why ever not, mun, it's only a step. I've been to England before now,' he'd said, refusing to recognize the nature of Josi's thanks.

Robin knew every farm, hamlet and pub on the way and kept up a lively flow of anecdotes about the more interesting of the inhabitants. Here a schoolmaster, here a publican, here a farmer or a farmer's wife had written a book or won a chair or found a bag of sovereigns or gone to the dogs. For most of the journey, he and Josi walked on in front to lighten the horses' load.

To Miriam, the journey was a highly emotional experience. She had long got used to the fact that she had taken another woman's husband, but the fact that she was literally taking him away from his wife, his children and their home seemed to be hitting her for the first time. What right had she to do so? For love? Could love be made responsible for all the upheaval and the hurt? How could Josi bear it? How could he bear to leave a place where he'd been master for over twenty years for a place where he would be a servant? How could he bear to leave his birthplace? 'That's Cefn Hebog,' she'd heard him tell Robin when they'd got a few miles outside Llanfryn. 'Hard country up there,' he'd said, a measure of pride in his voice. How could he walk with such an easy step, so complacently surveying the land he knew and loved and was leaving.

They were really climbing now, the mist-white river far below, wooded hills on each side of them, pink morning light on gnarled oak and ash. At last the mountain plateau where they could see half of Wales, it seemed, spread out before them; round-backed Plynlymon to the North, the ghost of Cader Idris beyond, Prescelly and the Brecon Beacons to the South and East.

'Well, isn't it a grand day,' Josi said, walking back a step or two to join her. 'We're going down as far as the Drovers Arms before we stop for breakfast. To get some shade for the horses. Look around you now. Isn't it like the top of the world?'

But Miriam was in despair. What right had she to find comfort in the beauty of a summer morning? ' "And Branwen looked on Ireland and the Island of the Mighty, what she might see of them",' she said at last, almost in a whisper. ' "Two good islands have been laid waste because of me. She heaved a great sigh and straightway broke her heart".'

'That's from the *Mabinogion*,' she told Josi after a moment or two.

'I know it,' he said. 'Had a sweetheart once, a school-mistress. Very elevating.'

'What became of her?' Miriam asked. But Josi had returned to Robin and the horses.

'Miriam here, had a lad from the Dolau starting school a while back. Just four years old. She was sitting at his side, showing him a picture-book of animals, getting him to name them for her, breaking him in, you might say. They come to a picture of a sheep; little fellow looks at it and hesitates. We've got a slow one here, she thinks. "Dammo," he said after a bit, "you've got me puzzling now. Is it a Clun Forest or a Suffolk? Not one of ours, anyhow." '

The baby slept.

It was ten o'clock when they halted. The sun was beginning to get hot, larks hung in the sky, when one stopped singing and descended, another began on the long thrilling ascent so that the song seemed endless. The sky was a golden haze.

They sat amongst buttercups and purple vetch and long slender grasses the colour of young apples, and ate bread and cheese and drank home-brewed from a stone jar.

Afterwards, the men took oats to the horses and Miriam nursed the baby. She took off her little sticky garments to let her feel the sun; it was the first time she had been out-of-doors; she waved her small arms about and kicked and lunged, drowning in a sea of air.

Josi came back alone, Robin bach was smoking his pipe and keeping out of their way for five minutes.

'You look like a gipsy with that scarf over your head and the wagon behind you,' Josi said.

Miriam shivered in the warmth of the morning. It was all too much for her. The tender breeze, the lovely grass; every blade was beautiful, every tiny flower. She picked a wild rose, so delicate its colour, shape and smell that she felt overwhelmed. What was its purpose? She crushed it in her hand. Only to ensure the future of the species, only to keep going the wheel of the seasons. It was heart-rending.

'What's it for, all this beauty?' she asked Josi.

'It's for the glory of God,' he said simply.

Miriam tossed her head, not angrily but sadly. 'Listen to that greenfinch calling to its mate in the hawthorn. Such tenderness. Not even a song, just a little, "Here I am", like you used to tap on my window. And when the fledglings are flown, they'll go their own ways again. Everything, and all of us, betrayed by the power of the mating drive. It's the cruelty of God, if you ask me.'

'That too,' Josi said. 'You can't separate the one from the other. Dark and light, light and shade, glory and cruelty; that's how it is. You mustn't fight it. It's no use.'

She looked at him with awe. To Josi everything was straight-forward. If only I could put my weight on the earth squarely as he does, she thought; make living as simple as breathing in and out. She put her hand on his chest, at the top, where his shirt was open.

'Wanton,' he said, turning towards her.

Pain rose to her heart, exquisitely, like the larks rising.

Then Robin came back towards them, leading the horses. Miriam dressed the baby and Josi helped her back into the wagon.

They travelled slowly because of the heat of the day.

'Is that the sea?' Miriam asked, sitting up so suddenly that she woke the baby. Everything in the distance was so blue that she couldn't be certain.

'Aye,' Robin bach said. 'Aye, that's it. That's the sea right enough.'

'We've arrived then,' Josi said. 'We turn off on this corner here.'

'We'll be near the sea then, will we?'

'A mile or two, I think.'

'Fancy forgetting to mention the sea.'

'I chose the place for the view,' Josi said, with a touch of irony. Then, in case he had been too severe, he sang a few lines of an old folk song.

> *On the seashore is a flat stone,*
> *Where my love and I would meet.*
> *Now the wild thyme grows about it*
> *And sprigs of rosemary.*

He was glad she seemed pleased about the sea. He doubted whether there was anything else about the mean little cottage to give her much pleasure.

'Well, here it is.'

It was an uncompromising box of a house, peeling whitewash under a slate roof, four small windows and a door, a holly tree outside, a square garden in front, a yard at the side, a woodshed, a pump and a clothes line.

'It's very homely,' Miriam said, as Josi lifted her and the baby out of the cart. She was pleased to find it so unprepossessing. A puritan streak in her nature wouldn't have wanted anything beyond her deserts. The morning had confounded her.

'I'll make you a seat here,' Josi said, marking the spot where he'd set her down with the palm of his hand. 'And you can sit and look at the sea.'

'I'll have to go up to the house for the door key,' he told Robin. 'I'll be back as soon as I can. Just up the road about a quarter of a mile; shouldn't take me long.'

'I don't like the old sea myself,' Robin said, as he took the horses out of the shafts. 'On a day like today, well, it looks harmless enough, but it's different in the winter when it starts churning about and reminding you of all the drowned. It's not alive like the land is; it doesn't produce anything, seed-time or harvest, except old fish. It just lies there skulking and churning about and reminding you.'

'I've only seen it once before,' Miriam said, as though to excuse her moment of excitement. 'Close to, I mean.'

'You're close enough to it here, in all conscience, but that doesn't mean to say you've got to go in or on it. As long as you don't go in it or on it, it can't do you too much harm, except like the river, it can go on your chest if you're prone, and if you are, chewing an onion last thing at night and first thing in the morning is the thing to do. Baby won't suffer though, you shall see, wrapped in it from infancy, she won't be prone.'

'I think I'll go and peep through the windows,' Miriam said, a little worried in case Robin felt it necessary to carry on talking until Josi came back.

'No, no, not for the world. Oh no. It'll bring you nothing but bad luck. There's nothing so unlucky as to see your future home for the first time through glass. Nothing in the world.'

Miriam expressed her thanks for his warning and stayed by his side.

'Not that I'm superstitious,' he told her, 'not in the least bit. Not on my own account. It's only the moon I'm careful of, especially with sowing seeds or planting potatoes. It's only a fool who ignores the moon. Aye indeed.'

Miriam moved the baby to her other arm. She was still fast asleep, drugged by the fresh air.

'Stop a minute now. Was your grandfather Ellis Lewis the cobbler in Cefnmwyn?'

'Yes he was. Did you know him?'

'No. But I knew one of his sons, Sam. Your uncle he'd be. He went down South to the pits with me thirty-odd years ago. Sam Lewis.'

'He's still down there, Aberdare way. I've never met him as far as I know, but I heard a lot about him from my mother.'

'He's still down there, then. He was courting Nel the daughter of The Coach-in-Hand when I knew him.'

'That's right. My Auntie Eleanor. She came to stay with us once. She'd been ill and she came to us afterwards.'

'A stout girl she was when I knew her.'

'I can't remember much about her, I'm afraid. It was years ago. Before my father died.'

'Yes, very stout and jolly. She would have made anyone a good wife. Sam was with the horses in the pits. Good little man, he was.'

'How long did you stay down there?'

'Three years exactly. Aye, indeed. It was work and the money was good but it was out of the light of day and besides I was promised to Let the Mill as she was then, and back I came. Not that the girls down South are not pretty, they are, diawch-i, and one or two of them did me the honour of asking me home after a bit of a walk we might have had out on the mountain. But a promise is a promise and Let was waiting and home I came, thirty-three years old with fifty gold sovereigns saved; enough in those days to buy two good horses and a wagon. Aye indeed. And fancy you being Sam Lewis's niece. Well, I'll tell you something, then. Since you are niece to old Sam, I'll let you into a secret. That man you've got there is one in ten thousand and don't let anyone tell you anything different. One and all, rich and poor; everyone is the same to Josi Evans. I've known him since he was a slip of a boy, mind. One in ten thousand. So there you are; you can be happy. And remember that anyone who casts a stone is not half the man Josi Evans is. Here he is now. Not a word. Not a word.'

'Have you two been talking about me?' Josi asked. 'Ruining my character?'

'Not at all. Saying I was that a ship — now, people are always praising the beauty of a ship — but saying I was that to me a ship isn't anywhere near as noble-looking as a plough. What do you say to that?'

'He's a bit of a poet,' Josi told Miriam. 'His father, Gwilym Cothi, was noted for it and it goes in families like a wall-eye.'

Josi unlocked the front door and they trooped into the house; Josi first, then Robin, and last Miriam and the baby.

It was the best kitchen they saw first; the paper peeling from the wall, the fireplace full of ash; a smell of damp soot; even in the midsummer heat, it was chilly. The kitchen was even worse, piled high with rubbish, old clothes and mattresses, discarded pots and pans and bottles, even old food to judge by the flies and the bitter, rancid smell.

'Whoever lived here before had a poorish notion of cleaning up,' Robin said.

'Chap was killed. Thrown off a horse, broke his back. The wife was in a bit of a state, no doubt.'

'Something else you didn't tell me,' Miriam said.

'Not many jobs going before Michaelmas.'

'Poor old fellow. It happens. Even among horses there'll be a bad one now and then.'

'What I'm concerned about now is why Isaac Lloyd didn't see fit to have someone clean up a bit before we arrived.'

'Too busy with the hay,' Robin said. 'Never mind, I'll stay and give you a hand. Drag it all outside, have a good fire. There's water in the pump so it's quite safe and there's not much in the garden to spoil. Go upstairs, my boy, and see what's there.'

The two rooms upstairs were bare and relatively clean.

The men started on the work.

Miriam fetched the Moses basket from the wagon and carried it upstairs, setting it down by the window in the larger of the two rooms. Then she changed the baby and laid her down in it. She cried so lustily, though, that she had to feed her again before she was able to go down to help. By the time she had finished, most of the rubbish was already in the garden. The fire the men lit lasted for over an hour and all the time it burned, Miriam thought of the man who'd been thrown off his horse and had died. It seemed a bad omen. She knew she should be cleaning the kitchen but couldn't begin on it. She stayed outside with Josi, feeding the fire, being near him. Being near him was to feel his strength.

Afterwards, when everything was burnt to a clean black ash, they fetched the food from the wagon and unloaded the table and chairs and ate outside in the garden; bread and ham and onions, and afterwards Josi made a fire in the kitchen grate and got their new kettle and made tea for Miriam while he and Robin finished the beer.

He and Miriam sat close together and later Robin smoked his pipe, and in the heat haze of the early afternoon when even the birds were silent they rested and took in their surroundings; the sea dazzling in front of them, the green hills behind, no sign of any other house, no noise except the whirring of the mowing machine in some unseen field; the smell of mint and blackcurrants and Robin's strong tobacco, the faint taste of salt on the tongue.

For the moment, Miriam felt at rest. All the guilt and discord and passion, like the noise of the million summer insects around her, dissolved into a low and peaceful hum.

All too soon, though, it was time to re-start work. They unloaded the wagon, setting everything down in the garden. Robin stayed to help Josi carry the bed upstairs and then he set off for home; Josi and Miriam standing in the road waving until he was out of sight. He had refused payment.

'It's my turn to work now,' Miriam said. 'I've got to clean out that kitchen before we can take anything inside. I've got my canvas apron and a scrubbing brush somewhere.'

'I've got a hatchet and a bill-hook somewhere, too. I need to chop some wood before I do anything else. Afterwards, I've got to go up to the house again to get my orders for tomorrow.'

Miriam swept the floor in every room and then began to scrub the flags of the best kitchen and the kitchen. She got a rag and washed the windows inside and out and every shelf upstairs and down. After that she turned her attention to the kitchen grate. She didn't have any blacking so had to be satisfied with rubbing it ferociously with an old piece of velvet. That done she sorted out the pots and pans, washing all the things which had been stored for months in Cefn Eithin's barn, and finding places for them in the pantry and on the wooden shelves near the grate. She brought in the hand-made rug Auntie Hetty had given them and then carried in the new table and chairs. She set the clock going and put it on the mantlepiece with the tea canister and the pair of brass candlesticks she'd received from her pupils. She polished her mother's armchair with some beeswax she found on a shelf in the pantry. She fetched kindling from the pile of wood Josi had chopped and made a fire. She went to the pump to fill the kettle and when she straightened herself she was so giddy from exhaustion and heat that she sat on the grass and wept.

Josi found her there when he returned from the farm.

'You're not strong enough for all this lifting and scrubbing,' he said, carrying her to the chair by the fire. 'And besides, that wasn't what I hired you for.'

There was nothing much more to do but feed the baby again and have some tea. Josi carried the small chest of drawers upstairs to their bedroom and then they had completed their move.

ELEVEN

The hay had been safely gathered in, and in record time, and the work of Hendre Ddu continued at a more leisurely pace.

In the second week of July the annual picnic was held in Garth Isa, the elm-fringed meadow by the river, but it was Catrin and Miss Rees who presided over the lavish tea for the workmen and their wives and children, Mrs Evans still being too weak to venture from the house.

Tom had hoped that Edward would be back for the picnic; the previous summer his presence had made it enjoyable for the first time for several years. But the letter he had sent reminding him of the date had remained unanswered; Tom had heard nothing from him since his hurried return to London almost a month earlier. Tom had had to organize the children's races instead of his father, take part in the tug-of-war and give the impression that he was enjoying himself. Life and picnics had to go on.

'If only I could see an improvement in Mrs Evans,' Miss Rees said, several times every day to anyone who would listen, 'I wouldn't worry about anything else.'

Tom envied the old woman her whole-hearted loyalty. He seemed to have many worries, large and small.

One of the things on his mind was the debts he had managed to run up over the last academic year, not enormous ones, but large enough to cause him anxiety. The previous summer he had been able to settle his, admittedly smaller, debts from the money his father had given him for his holiday. 'How much will you be wanting?' his father had asked, and though his eyes had widened when Tom had named a sum sufficient to clear his debts as well as cover the week in London, he had handed it over without a word.

'You see, I owe a bit, here and there,' Tom had explained. 'Well, you have to stand your friends a lunch now and then, don't you? You can't stop them dropping in to your rooms for drinks, can you?'

He knew he couldn't begin to explain his debts to his mother. She thought his allowance very generous and would be hurt, even horrified, to know that he had over-spent it and without asking her permission.

A hundred, a hundred and fifty, was nothing, he told himself, compared to what several of his friends owed to various tradesmen. He was already twenty-one, and since he was going to remain home to run the farm he would be able to insist on a decent allowance and would be able to get everything sorted out before too long.

But whenever he managed to console himself, he remembered his father's letter; how he had seemed so concerned about a twenty pounds he had taken from the bank before leaving home, his promise to repay it before Michaelmas.

Before he could approach his mother for money for himself, he knew that he must tackle the matter of his father's loan; he couldn't bear to think that he might he harassed by such a trivial sum. What did they know of the stresses and strains of his new life?

By the Sunday evening following the picnic he had become so worried and depressed that he knew he had to talk to his mother. She had had a relatively good day, had been to morning service for the first time for weeks and had got up again after her afternoon rest.

He went for a walk by the river after tea, rehearsing what he was going to say; he had never before interfered with anything which wasn't, strictly speaking, his concern. When he got back, he found her alone in the drawing-room reading her Bible.

The drawing-room was an ugly, over-furnished room, not much used. There were dark oil paintings of his grandfather and great-grandfather and other members of the Morgan family all around on the dark, maroon and brown wallpaper, and old sepia photographs in heavily decorated frames on every available surface. Most rooms in the farmhouse had retained a Georgian simplicity, but the drawing-room was Victorian; plush and velvet and mahogany. Only Christmas ever managed to lighten its gloom; in high summer it seemed particularly depressing.

Tom sat at the window so that he could look out at the trees and the sky, and waited for a sign that his mother was ready to talk to him. She went on reading her Bible as though unaware of his presence. It was only his determination to get at least one matter off his chest that kept him seated; he felt more uncomfortable by the minute.

'Tom,' she said at last, closing her Bible and taking off her glasses.

'I've been thinking about that letter Father sent,' Tom said, speaking hurriedly and rather too loudly in his embarrassment. 'He said he'd taken some money from the bank and intended paying it back as soon as he could.'

He faltered as she turned her large, down-drooping eyes on him. She seems to have cried away all the colour from her eyes, he thought, sadly; they used to be such a pretty blue.

'Have you given it any thought?' he continued lamely.

'How can I think about money at a time like this? Haven't I got enough on my mind?'

'Of course you have. Might it be better if I wrote to him – I've got his address – and told him he needn't pay it back? Tell him you said so.'

'Why? Is he in trouble?'

'I don't think so. Not as far as I know. But poor enough, I should think. Twenty pounds would make a lot of difference to him, I should think.'

Mrs Evans closed her eyes. Her hands were resting on the Family Bible which was on the circular table in front of her. Tom wondered if she was praying, asking for guidance. He felt near it himself.

'I can't let you do that,' she said at last. 'How can I, Tom? I would be condoning his sin if I provided money for him. I'm trying to keep my feelings out of the situation, imagining him a man married to a woman I don't even know. However desperate his plight, I couldn't condone his breaking his marriage vows.'

'You can't keep yourself out of it,' Tom said. 'How can you? No one can be objective about something so close to them. But I can't see that letting him keep that paltry sum of money is condoning anything. And legally I'm not even certain that he isn't entitled to keep it.'

His mother spun round to face him. 'Of course he's legally entitled to keep it,' she said angrily. 'I'm not interested in the legal position, you should know that. He drew whatever he wanted from my bank account and no questions asked, the money was as much his as mine, it was he that managed it, you know that very well. But he knows that he is not morally entitled to take money to ... to ... well, for sinful purposes, and if he hasn't lost all his moral values he will pay it back, and it's right that he should. It's a matter of conscience. Don't you understand?'

'Yes, I suppose so.' Tom spoke wearily, his sympathy for his mother worn very thin.

Suddenly, though, her tone changed completely.

'Tom, write to your father, you say you have his address, and ask him to come back. Tell him that if he comes home, I will provide generously, most generously, for the child. He can't think I would deny an innocent child. Oh Tom, if he understood that, and understood how I feel towards him, he would come home, I'm sure of it. I think he will come home, Tom, and so does Nano.'

Tom came over from the window, knelt by his mother and stroked her knees. He couldn't bear to look at her. He knew she was crying. And he couldn't bear to see her in tears, her face red and shapeless. He stayed where he was, his head on her knees, till she seemed to grow calmer.

'I'll try to be a good son to you,' he said. He felt uncomfortable at having to say such trite words. His being a good son was as inevitable as his being a good farmer, but he knew that she appreciated the expression of even the most obvious truths.

'I know you will.' She seemed relatively composed. But as he tried to rise from his knees, she suddenly grasped him about the shoulders again in a grip which hurt. 'Oh Tom, I want him back. I want you to get him back. I suppose you think I should have some pride, but I haven't any, Tom, none at all.'

He had to use some force to get away from her. She thought it was his sympathy for her which made him rush out of the room, and indeed he did feel a tearing, humiliating pity. But his strongest feeling was anger. He was angry with both his parents.

He went up to his bedroom at the back of the house, shut the door and leaned against it. He could hear the cows lowing gently as they were turned out of the milking-sheds. After a few moments he went over to the window and raised it as high as it would go. He could hear Davy shouting as the cows loitered under the low branches of the elder trees in the lane that led to Cae Gwyn. He could smell the heavy sweetness of the elder flower. There was thunder in the air.

'Confound everything,' he said. He was amazed at the whirlwind of anger and self-pity in his head; he always thought of himself as calm and reasonable. He remained staring out of the window until the sky darkened and the first rain came.

'Could you let me have twenty pounds?' he asked Miss Rees the next morning. He had convinced himself that it was of the utmost importance to let his father have the money he owed his mother as soon as possible.

'I could,' Miss Rees said, 'but I know that if it was money you ought to have, you'd ask your mother for it, so I won't.'

'You're a hard woman, Nano. I'll have to go to a money-lender, and he'll probably ruin me.'

'Have your breakfast first.'

She thought he was teasing her, and in a way he was. He hadn't expected money from Miss Rees, would probably not have accepted it had it been offered. He wanted her sympathy, he supposed; wanted to interest her in his financial problems. But she wasn't having any of it. She sailed across the room with his bacon and eggs, quite above money matters.

'You're the only one in the world I love, Nano,' he said, seizing her large, rough hands in his.

'I don't want any of that nonsense, Mr Tom,' she said severely, pulling away from him. 'For shame. A grown man.'

Catrin came in to the morning-room and Miss Rees left her to pour out Tom's second cup of tea.

'What a storm last night,' Catrin said. 'Did you sleep? I was up with Mother. She's terrified of thunder. We were awake half the night. She's asleep now, though, I think.'

Tom stared at Catrin. 'You're very patient with her,' he said. 'You're much better to her than I am.'

Catrin drank a cup of tea and stared back at Tom as though not recognising him.

I fell in love with Edward because he was there, she told herself. Because I needed to be in love, not because it was fated or because he was anyone special. I wanted to feel. I wanted to suffer. I was in waiting. I needed him. As the earth needs rain, I needed him so that my awakened senses could root and leaf. I love him. I love him.

'Do you want marmalade?' she asked Tom. 'Or gooseberry jam? Lowri made this from the first little berries. The young fruit sets without needing too much sugar. Isn't the colour lovely? Goosegog green. Like little frogs.'

She held the glass dish up to the window.

'It's too sour for me,' Tom said. 'I tried some yesterday.'

'Lowri got a prize for it in the Henblas Fruit and Vegetable Show. One pound of gooseberry preserve. I'll tell Nano you don't like it. She *will* be pleased.'

She got up, fetched a tray and started to load it.

'I don't understand you,' Tom said as she was leaving the room. 'You seem light-headed.'

'Isn't it the limit, though,' he said to Miss Rees later on. 'She's nagged about going to Art School ever since she left school and the moment Mother and I agree to her going she seems to have got cold feet.'

'Better to change her mind now than go all the way to London and change afterwards. It's seeing a bit of sense she is, if you ask me.'

'Is it because Mother isn't very well?'

'It may be that, it may not.'

Miss Rees was the only one who had guessed about Edward Turncliffe's part in Catrin's change of heart.

'Isn't Mr Turncliffe supposed to be coming back for the harvest? Has he said when he's coming?'

'No, he hasn't given a definite date. Why?'

'He's a pleasant young man, Mr Turncliffe. Is he rich, say?'

I don't think so. Not Lady Harris rich.'

'Does a lawyer get more money than a doctor?'

'You can't generalize. Are you match-making, Nano, by any chance? Because if you are, I think you ought to know...'

But as Tom was about to tell Nano about Rose Fletcher, Edward's fiancée, Catrin came back, a little breathlessly, to ask whether the postman had been.

'Yes, he's been,' Nano said. 'Nothing for you, though. Nor for Mr Tom either. Nothing but a parcel of linen for Mrs Evans.'

97

Catrin went out again without another word.

'What's the matter with her?' Tom asked. 'Has she got a sweetheart? Or is she expecting a letter from Father?'

'Why don't you ask her, Mr Tom? Why don't you *talk* to her? She's worried about something, that I do know, she's eating almost as little as Mrs Evans; we could keep both of them on a preacher's salary. Why don't you take the two of them to Tenby for a few days, now that the hay is in? Miss Owen, Bodlondeb, would be so pleased to see you again. And wasn't there a bit of courting going on there last year? Not that old Nano expects to know anything except from hearsay and guessing.'

'There was nothing, Nano, nothing at all. If there was, you'd be the first to hear of it, I promise you. Yes, all right, there was a young lady staying at Bodlondeb last year, a Miss Bevan-Walters who was the daughter of some big coal owner and so of a certain interest to my mother. She wasn't ugly or crippled apart from that I remember nothing about her very clearly except for the extraordinary way she ate grapes; she made a little tunnel of her hand and shot the pips out through it on to her plate. Very fancy.'

'She went to Horeb morning and evening according to Mrs Evans. Mrs Evans was very impressed by that. It's very unusual, she said, for any young lady nowadays to go twice a Sunday while she's on holiday. Unless she's *very* devout.'

'Or unless she takes a fancy to the minister. Idris Williams, Horeb, is a handsome man, Nano, and a bachelor.'

'So is Thomas Evans, Hendre Ddu.'

'You want to find a wife for me, is that it?'

'No hurry in the world, Mr Tom. Having a nice young lady would do for a start. Just a bit of excitement for us all. Though I must say I do want to see a wife and heir here before I shut my old eyes.'

'Let me know, then, if there's someone you think might suit. No, I mean it. I'd appreciate your help.'

'Who do I ever see, Mr Tom, of the right standing for you?'

'Never mind about the right standing. A bit of money behind her is what I want, and the look of a breeder.'

'If you're going to talk like that, I'll get on with my work. You go after Miss Catrin and draw her out a bit. And keep the talk decent, now; she doesn't need any encouragement.'

Tom had no intention of following Catrin, but almost immediately came across her in the orchard where he had gone to do some scything. She was sitting on the seat there, her hands in her lap, looking so utterly miserable, so frozen and immobile with grief, that his heart lurched with sympathy. 'Catrin,' he said. 'Whatever is the matter? You must tell me.'

'There's nothing the matter. Nothing at all. I've got a bit of a headache. Nothing else.'

She got up and left him.

Perhaps it was just a headache, Tom thought, that and the strain of the past weeks. He wished she would confide in him as she did in Edward. Why did she no longer want to go to college? If only Edward would come back as he'd promised to. They hadn't heard a word from him. Was it because he had appeared rather curt and unfriendly towards him? Surely he'd have realized that it was the pressure he was under. He'd write to him again.

Before he had finished sharpening the scythe, he heard the doctor's car in the drive and hurried to catch him before he went upstairs to his mother.

'I'm a bit worried about Catrin,' he said. 'She's looking terrible and Miss Rees has been complaining that she doesn't eat. I wish you'd see her.'

'Send her up to me.'

'What will I say? You know how stubborn she is.'

'Tell her I want a word with her about Mrs Evans.'

After Doctor Andrews had spent five or ten minutes with his patient, he went in to the morning-room to look for Catrin. Miss Rees heard him there and came in from the kitchen.

'Where is Miss Evans? I'd like to see her a moment.'

'I'm not sure. She's out somewhere. I'll send one of the girls after her.'

'Thank you. I'll wait.'

Doctor Andrews sat on the window-seat, pulling out his watch as he did so. He had several calls that morning; all the same he would stay to see Catrin.

Not that he was worried about her. It was natural for young girls to take things badly, to lose their appetites, to fret and pine and languish, especially highly-charged, emotional girls like her.

The previous winter he had seriously considered asking Catrin to marry him; he was a widower and not getting any younger, and she was both lovely and accessible. They had met on several occasions, dinners and parties, around Christmas time, and it was only the over-emotional streak in her nature which had made him decide against it. He felt that she would be too much for him to take on, would prove more than he could manage. He was a hard-working man who loved his profession and what he wanted above all was companionship. No, that wasn't true, he wanted love, too, but a moderate love. He felt that she would either claim too much of his life, or complicate matters even more by falling in love with someone else. And nothing by halves.

Since knowing of her father's disastrous misalliance, he felt doubly sure that he had made the right decision; Hendre Ddu was all right but the Evans blood was intemperate. All the same, he had retained an affectionate interest in her. He sat and waited.

'I'm, sorry to have kept you,' she said when she came in a few minutes later, 'I didn't know you were here. How is Mother?'

'How are you? Come here, I want to have a look at you.'

He turned her towards the window. How unfair it was that young girls looked even more beautiful when they were miserable and unable to sleep, whereas their mothers became haggard and ugly.

'Are you going to Art School in September?'

'No. I've decided against it.'

'Why?'

She shrugged her shoulders. 'I've decided that the world can do without my artistic gifts,' she said lightly.

Then her mood changed. 'I want to be a nurse. Do you think that's possible?'

'I've no idea whether your parents would allow it. It's very strenuous work. Whatever made you think of being a nurse?'

Doctor Andrews sighed. He guessed it was a gesture of self-sacrifice; an Irish girl would have been thinking of taking the veil, he supposed.

'I want to do something worthwhile. I enjoy painting and drawing, but I've got no real talent. It wouldn't do anyone any good.'

He looked at her for a long time without speaking. Who did she imagine herself in love with?

'I think there's more to it than you're prepared to tell me.'

'Perhaps there is. But I really want to be a nurse. Could you help me?'

She laid her hand on his arm and turned her eyes on him with anguished appeal. It was the sort of exaggerated emotion which had warned him off.

'I'll speak to your mother and Tom. I certainly think you'd make a good nurse if you could stand the hardship.'

'Oh, I could. When will you speak to them?'

'I haven't any time now, my dear. I'm already late.'

'Could you come to dinner tonight? Or tomorrow night? Tom is free, I know.'

'Very well. Thank you. Tomorrow night. I'll see what I can do for you then.'

'I'd rather she went to Art School if she has to go anywhere,' Tom said. He had eaten well. Cold salmon and steak and kidney pie. Fresh, wholesome food, well-cooked and not messed about, that's what he liked.

He looked at Catrin. She was wearing a plain, dark blue blouse as though to impress them with the seriousness of her intentions, Even her hair had been scraped back as though to fit under a nurse's cap.

'What do you think, Mrs Evans?' the doctor asked.

His mother had on one of her beautiful lace dresses, in honour of the doctor, perhaps. Her face was paler than the dress.

'I don't know. Nursing is a wonderful job, but she'd see some terrible sights.'

'Shall I tell you why I think she'd make a good nurse?'

Doctor Andrews was playing for effect. He let them wonder for a few moments. Everyone looked at Catrin. Her spoon rattled nervously against her glass bowl of raspberries. She tried to smile.

'Because her mother is such a good nurse.'

Catrin almost clapped her hands with pleasure.

Rachel Evans coloured delicately. 'I am?'

'You. A very devoted and dedicated nurse. I shan't forget how you nursed Miss Rees through pneumonia a few years ago. And against my orders too. Do you remember? When I said the night nursing was too much for you and arranged for Mrs Prosser to take it over, do you remember what happened? I do. Mrs Prosser was trusted to do a few hours morning and afternoon when the patient was easier, and you stayed up every night for a week. Yes, and I remember you when Tom had concussion too and when Catrin had scarlet fever. A born nurse, I've said so, many times.'

'You're trying to get round me,' Mrs Evans said.

'Perhaps I am, but only with the truth.'

'It will have to be thought about very carefully. I'm not at all sure if she's strong enough to bear the long hours. It's very good of you, Doctor Andrews, to interest yourself in Catrin's future.'

Tom would have been much happier had the doctor's interest in his sister's future taken another direction. The last time he was home he'd felt sure the fellow was in love with her. He looked at them both. What had happened? Had she turned him down? Catrin was a complete mystery to him. One moment she seemed as giddy as a schoolgirl, the next she was begging to be allowed to dedicate her life to nursing.

The talk turned to other subjects, but when Catrin could see that her mother was getting tired, and realized that she would at any moment excuse herself from the company, she made another effort to advance her cause.

'Could I train at Carmarthen Hospital, Doctor Andrews? So that I'd be near home.'

'Cardiff General Infirmary would be the place. They have a well-established training school there.'

'Cardiff is very far away,' Mrs Evans said wearily. 'I really don't know what to say.'

When Catrin had taken her mother to bed, Tom sat waiting for the doctor to begin working on him, but to his surprise he remained silent.

'Of course, I'd much prefer it if she just stayed home,' Tom said, to start the ball rolling.

'Let her go away,' Doctor Andrews said. He lowered his eyes and pulled his chair closer to Tom's. 'How soon before she comes down?'

'She's usually about a quarter of an hour. Why? What's the matter?'

'I've got some bad news for you, Tom. Tom, I'm afraid your mother is dying.'

Tom said nothing. The certainty in the doctor's voice stunned him. All he could do was to stare unblinkingly in his face.

'She can't live more than six months. It will probably be considerably less.'

Tom still said nothing.

'I'd like Catrin to be away. Do you understand? Tom?'

'How do you *know*?'

'There isn't any doubt, I'm afraid. I got Harcourt-Jones, the top man, out here a few months ago when I wasn't absolutely certain. He confirmed my diagnosis. By this time, though, any first year medical student could tell you the same thing.'

'Are you equally certain about... ?'

'Yes. Equally certain. Three to six months. I'm sorry to have to break it to you tonight, but she'll soon be unable to get up at all and it will be time we talked about getting a nurse.'

'I think Catrin should stay with her.'

'I think she should be away, Tom, and I know best about that.'

'So she won't be told?'

'Not until much nearer the end.'

Tom was suddenly struck by a vivid memory of his mother as a young woman. He was out walking with Nano, probably two or three at the time. His mother had appeared in front of them. On horseback. Riding side-saddle. A dark blue costume. She'd waved at him, smiled, and ridden on. He could remember the anguish he'd felt as she had disappeared round a bend in the road. He could remember screaming and kicking. He could remember Nano recounting the incident later, 'He can't bear to let her out of his sight.' He could still feel the hard, convulsive sob, the pain in his throat.

'I was on the point of breaking the news to your father when I found he'd left home. If I hadn't delayed so long, he wouldn't have gone, I suppose.'

'Wouldn't he?'

'Surely not. He wouldn't have left a dying wife. God, how I blame myself. I didn't entertain the possibility of his leaving home. I knew about the woman. Even about the baby. Yet I had no inkling that he could intend breaking up his home for them; leaving

103

his wife and family. It's something outside my experience.'

Doctor Andrews left the table and went to stand by the window. He hadn't expected telling Tom to prove so difficult. He'd forgotten how young he was.

'Perhaps he'd come back,' Tom said.

The doctor shrugged his shoulders. Joshua Evans was completely beyond his understanding. The best farm in the area. A gracious and charming wife. Beyond understanding.

'Perhaps he'd come back if I told him how things were. Mother wanted me to write asking him to come back; wanted me to tell him that she would provide for the baby. I know where he's gone. I could go over to see him. If he knows it's only a matter of months, he'd come back. Wouldn't he?'

'I honestly don't know.'

'What would he lose? As you said, he wouldn't have gone if he'd known the circumstances. Surely he'll come back since it's for such a short time? Won't he? What's the woman like? Miss Lewis?'

Doctor Andrews didn't answer because he'd heard Catrin coming downstairs. He turned to warn Tom of her arrival. When she came in, the doctor was still at the window, looking out into the darkness.

'Well, he's got round me,' Tom told Catrin. 'I've been over-ruled. You'll have to get him to talk to Miss Rees as well, Catrin, I don't think she's going to take it very well.'

'And now, I must be on my way,' Doctor Andrews said.

Catrin stared at him. She had never known him so abrupt. There was a strange atmosphere in the room. Unease.

'Thank you for taking my part,' she said, giving him her hand.

The doctor seemed almost reluctant to take it. However he did, pressed it, looked at her hard for a moment and then left, Tom taking him to the door.

TWELVE

Rose Fletcher, Edward's fiancée, was the only child of doting, elderly parents.

Up to the age of fourteen she had been educated at home by a conscientious but dull governess. When she was fourteen, though, her father's youngest brother, her uncle Charlie, had happened to visit them. He had a large family; three sons and three daughters, and had been appalled by his niece's lonely life. He begged her parents to let her finish her education at the school his daughters attended; he was sure, he said, that she was taught efficiently at home, but managed to persuade them that companionship with other girls would help develop her character and make her more out-going; better fitted for the pace of life in the twentieth century.

After a week or two's deliberation, her mother and father visited the school, and though they disapproved of the ugly uniform and the games they were most favourably impressed by the character of the headmistress, Miss Margaret Donnington, a young graduate with a deep hypnotic voice and a warm smile. She was not at all what they had expected.

They were completely won over when they met their nieces who seemed so happy and robust compared to their grave daughter. They made arrangements there and then for Rose to join her cousins after the summer holidays.

At the time, Rose, who was extremely shy and timid, had been dismayed; the only girls she ever came into contact with were those she met at the dancing class her governess took her to on Saturday mornings.

That she settled down so quickly and happily was due to her cousin Claire who took her under her wing.

Claire was a few months older than Rose and an exceptionally clever girl. She was also very attractive, with a warm, engaging personality. She had many friends competing for her attention, but she dropped them all in favour of her shy little cousin. Naturally, Rose idolized her.

Claire was determined to go to university like her brothers, and in order to keep up with her, Rose worked harder than anyone in the school; she was very far behind, particularly in maths and Latin.

At sixteen she was allowed to follow Claire to the upper sixth. She was careful, though, not to tell her parents that it was the form for those sitting their University Entrance.

In the sixth, Miss Donnington the Headmistress took over their History lessons. Under her influence – she was a socialist and a feminist – both girls became absorbed in current affairs and were able to see books and tracts on the Women's Movement, then at the height of its power, which would certainly not have come their way in other schools.

By the time Rose's parents had realized where Miss Donnington and Claire were leading their daughter, it was too late: she had dedicated herself to the cause.

They were adamant, though, that Rose should not go to university. They managed to persuade both the Headmistress and Rose herself that it was her duty to leave school to be with her mother, who was in her late fifties and delicate. Claire went to Somerville College, Oxford, and though the girls corresponded, Rose's parents did everything possible to prevent them meeting.

Rose never fulfilled the role of decorative drawing-room daughter that her mother had intended. The high sense of duty inculcated by the school comprised a duty to herself and society as well as to her parents. Her shapely nose was usually in a book or pamphlet and she insisted on attending meetings of the Women's Social and Political Union; threatened to run away from home and become a stenographer or shop assistant if they tried to stop her.

Left to herself, Rose would have shown no interest in young men. Edward, though, she had known all her life, and since he was by this time a serious student preparing to go up to Oxford, she found his company interesting and stimulating and they were soon good friends. Within a few months he was taking Claire's place in her life.

Some months later, after Rose had accepted Edward's proposal of marriage, her father felt much happier about her. He agreed to her devoting some time to the cause of women's suffrage on condi-

106

tion that she would not involve herself in any illegal action without consulting him and obtaining his permission. Rose decided that she had no right to disobey her father until she was twenty-one, when, due to an annuity left her by her grandmother, she would no longer be completely dependent on him. At that time she would tell him that she intended to act entirely according to her conscience.

So for two years she had stood at street corners selling 'Votes for Women', addressed envelopes, washed dishes after celebration meetings, and bided her time.

During those years she didn't doubt that she could and would be a heroine when her time came. When she saw women newly released from prison, pale and thin from weeks of thirst and starvation fasts, and heard their descriptions of being seized and bound and forcibly fed, she thought the emotion she felt was horror for their treatment, not fear.

As soon as she was twenty-one she informed her parents that she intended to volunteer for disruptive work, and by this time, knowing how much in earnest she was, they realized that it would be in vain to try to forbid her. Her father admired her spirit although he worried a great deal about her. Her mother neither approved nor understood.

For five or six weeks Rose was not involved in dangerous work. At the time, there was hope that a bill concerning women's suffrage would be brought before parliament, and whilst there was a chance of its being successful the militants had pledged themselves to a period of non-violence.

In June, though, due to the failure of the bill, the temperature was at fever pitch again, and she was chosen as one of three women to set fire to the empty country house of one of the prominent anti-suffrage MPs. Arson was the thing she particularly dreaded. All the same she followed her instructions carefully and well; at that stage, able to fight her repugnance and fear. After the ordeal of ensuring that the house was completely empty and getting the fire well and truly lit, she and her two companions were duly arrested.

She had expected it and had prepared herself for every step of the subsequent proceedings; all the same, the reality had been too much for her. Even the policeman's grip on her wrists as he had jerked and pulled her roughly to the waiting Black Maria had been unbearable. Crowds had jeered as she and her companions were taken from the van to Cannon Row Police Station. Eggs had been thrown at them and a pleasant-looking young man had spat in her face. After only one night in the cells, filthy and evil-smelling, her nerve had failed her. The thought of having to endure a prison sentence filled her with panic. She tried to steady her mind by thinking of what the leaders had suffered; Mrs Pankhurst herself had been in prison nine times, enduring every humiliation; the others, one or two of them almost as young and frail-looking as she herself, had been released from prison almost at the point of death, only to defy the police by taking part in a further demonstration on the very first day of freedom. She thought about these women she so admired until tears ran down her cheeks, but their shining example failed to sustain her. She could admire, but couldn't follow. All she wanted was her liberty at any cost. Her faith in herself was completely and utterly shattered.

This was the poor frightened creature, more pitiable since she had previously been so brisk and brave, so forceful and determined, that Edward was taken to see when he returned to London. He was moved to tears.

Rose's father, his own father's business partner and dearest friend, had met him at Paddington to put him in the picture. Rose had confessed that she would do anything to get out of serving the prison sentence she had thought to undergo with such cheerful stoicism. Now, while she was in such a reasonable frame of mind, could Edward not press for an earlier marriage and take her to Oxford out of harm's way? Since he was twenty-three, there would be no difficulty in getting the college authorities to agree to his living outside; her father knew a man who knew the Dean; everything could be arranged. Rose was an only child and her father assured him that he would never regret the loss of his last year as a bachelor.

That was his duty, then. Edward could have as soon turned his back on a wounded child.

The next morning he was taken to the court and introduced to the barrister, who agreed that Rose's plans for imminent marriage would greatly enhance the likelihood of her being released with a caution.

That afternoon, when Rose, free again as the barrister had predicted – it was her first offence – was in her own bed trying to

108

recover from her ordeal, Edward and his future father-in-law had bought a special licence and arranged for the wedding.

The terrible doubts of his first evening at home had been partly dispelled on the second evening, spent alone with Rose – it was the first time they had ever been allowed so much time on their own – when he had found that the excitement which had engulfed him in Catrin's presence was by no means absent when he was with Rose. And she was so nearly his; that in itself was thrilling, there would be no years of waiting; meeting and parting. And everyone was so happy and so pleased with them both. And besides, he had no choice. He had no choice.

In the depths of his mind, he realized that regrets would catch up with him, that he was being false to the revelation he had had of his own nature, but for the most part he was swept along on a tide of sensual well-being. He still thought of Catrin, he couldn't help himself, but more and more she seemed a beautiful dream; seemed to inhabit the green fields of a dream.

It was three weeks before he could bring himself to write to her.

> My too-beautiful Catrin,
> Your anger bewitched me. Your slanting eyes were my undoing. So that I behaved in a way alien to my nature, in a way I feel deeply ashamed about. Please forgive me.
> I hope you will think of me always as
> > Your devoted friend,
> > > Edward Turncliffe.

It was over-written and artificial. Edward intended it to be so. He didn't want to get too near the bare truth.

Catrin received the letter without emotion. It was only the confirmation of the truth she already knew. She had never allowed herself to believe that Edward loved her.

Even at that moment when he had pulled her towards him in the trap and kissed her and she had felt for the first time sensations which had bewildered her by their intensity, she had known that the love he was professing wasn't love, but the other thing. He loved Rose.

But how sweet it had seemed, how right. They had looked at each other and had seemed to find the whole world. She felt almost giddy again at the memory of that look. And then the striving to get closer, her body melting. But the way that they had looked at each other had seemed a perfect thing; wide-eyed as they kissed they had seemed to be promising each other unknown certainties. Seemed. Seemed.

'Is it your brother's friend that you're mooning about?' Doctor Andrews asked her abruptly one morning after his now daily visit to her mother.

'There's nothing between us,' she had said, before she could think of denying the charge.

'That's not what I asked you.'

'Oh, please don't tease. Don't you realize how depressed I am about everything.'

Doctor Andrews was moved by her distress.

'But if I'm going to get you into the nursing profession, I have a right to know that you won't let me down by behaving like a love-sick schoolgirl.'

'I won't let you down, I promise you. When will you get in touch with the hospital?'

'I have. I wrote to the matron three days ago and had a reply this morning. She wants to know if you can be ready to go at the end of next week. She happens to have a vacancy on the course; she's sorry it's so little notice.'

'That's marvellous. I can't tell you how grateful I am.'

A weight seemed to have been lifted from Catrin's heart. She felt an upsurge of happiness which at once relayed itself to the doctor.

'But can they let you go before the corn harvest?'

'Yes. Lowri's youngest sister is leaving school this month and she's coming to be the little maid. Sali will take over the eggs and do my share of the dairy work, and more; I don't do much, Mother doesn't like it. And Sali's mother who does the washing can come most days, and Davy's wife and old Beti Pryce when they're needed. They won't miss me.'

'No farmer will marry you, you know, if you haven't had experience of running a farm house.'

'No. Lowri is the natural choice here, I'm afraid. Benji Brynmoel is already looking her over; that one-horse place of his has killed two wives already but he doesn't seem to have any objection to human sacrifice.'

'You're a hard woman, Catrin. Benji has two small children to bring up. How can he manage without a wife? He certainly doesn't spare himself. He works all hours of daylight and then goes to bed to save a candle. He'll go bankrupt if he doesn't have a wife to help him.'

'He shan't have Lowri, anyway, I'm determined on that. I'm against marriage.'

They were silent for a moment. Then the doctor opened his bag.

'I've got the forms you have to fill in. Your mother will have to sign one or two of them and send the money for your uniform; they'll kit you out when you get there as long as everything is paid for. You go up now and let her know about it. Tell her how lucky you were to get a place for this year; the course started in May, you know, but you'll soon catch up.'

He walked out to his car and cranked it up. He had been a houseman at Cardiff Infirmary and the matron, then a young sister, had been a particular friend of his.

Before going upstairs to her mother, Catrin went to find Lowri. Since she was leaving so soon, she needed to feel certain that Lowri would be staying. Her mother was very fond of her. Everyone was. She was a plump, good-natured girl with delicate pink cheeks and chestnut-coloured hair and eyes.

'I'm going away, Lowri, to be a nurse. Only you mustn't tell Miss Rees, yet, or anyone.'

Lowri's eyes widened at the secret she was the first to hear.

The back kitchen was cool even in the heat of July, and smelled of herbs and bacon. Catrin looked about her, for the first time conscious of things she would miss; the cool back kitchen, the sun slanting in from the small, high window, the uneven blue flags on the floor, the baskets of fruit and vegetables.

'You'll be housekeeper here when Miss Rees goes, you know that, don't you?'

'Where is Miss Rees going?'

'When she's too old to work, I mean.'

'Miss Rees. She'll never be too old to work. Not till she drops. She'll still be holding the reins on her death bed, Miss Rees will.

Housekeeper indeed. I'll be biding my time for twenty years.'

'Aren't you happy here, Lowri?'

'Oh yes, I'm happy enough. I've been here ever since I came from school. Everyone's good to me. Even Miss Rees most of the time.'

'You're not thinking of leaving to get married?'

Lowri's round cheeks became a brighter pink at the suggestion.

'I'm not even walking out with anyone. I never have done.'

'You won't leave us, will you, Lowri?'

'Dear, dear, it's *you* that's leaving *us*. First Mr Evans and now you. Oh, I shouldn't have said that, Miss Catrin, Mr Evans will be back I'm sure, and before the harvest too. I said to Jâms only last night, 'Don't you get too big for your boots, Mister Muck, Mr Evans will surprise us all and come back any day now, and then he'll be lead horse again.'

'In any case, Tom will be staying on here. Only that's another secret, mind.'

Lowri's face flooded with colour again. 'Leaving the college and staying home to farm?'

Catrin nodded. 'So you won't leave us, will you? He'll need all the help he can get.'

'Of course I won't leave. Never.'

'Not even if Benji Brynmoel asks you to marry him?'

'That run-down old tramp. Not likely.'

Lowri suddenly gave a little gasp and rushed to the oven in the front kitchen. She brought out a large golden cake, perfectly risen and smelling of eggs and spice. She carried it carefully to the back kitchen, laying it down with the batch of fruit tarts she had made earlier. Catrin watched her. 'You're a wonderful cook, Lowri.'

'Quite good,' Lowri said truthfully. 'My bread isn't as good as Miss Rees's though. She says it takes fifty years to get the dough just right.'

Both girls felt the weight of fifty years on them for a moment.

Catrin was the first to shrug them off.

'If you and Jâms were to come to any agreement, Tom would find you a little place, you can depend on it. In six or seven years, say.

'Huh,' Lowri said. 'Huh.'

Catrin went upstairs to her mother.

'Why didn't Nano ever get married?' she asked her.

'Why should she get married? She had everything she wanted here. She was housekeeper before she was thirty. She's been here fifty-two years, a few weeks longer than I have. She came to be my nurse-maid.'

'I know.'

'When my poor mother died, and I only five at the time, who would have snatched Nano from me then?'

'Did anyone try? Did she ever have a sweetheart?'

'She may have done. I never heard of anyone. Perhaps she hoped my poor father would marry her. That sort of thing happens now and again, and oftener too, but he was a very proud man, my father, The Morgans were real gentry once, you know; they had large estates in Pembrokeshire at one time; I'm talking now of several generations back. I suppose he might have thought, at first, of marrying some rich English lady, but he must have lost heart. He didn't have any spirit for anything but work towards the end. Nano stayed with him, anyway.'

'She stayed with you, surely.'

'That's what I mean.'

'But you think she may have been in love with Grandfather.'

'In love? I don't know about that. She was a grown woman by the time I was old enough to take notice, not a girl. In any case, she was much better off here than she would have been in any small place with five or six children to rear.'

'I hope she thought so.'

'Of course she did. Well, I suppose she did. Some would choose poverty, I suppose. I don't feel certain of anything by this time. Why do you bother me?'

'I'm sorry. I'm very thoughtless.'

When Catrin told her mother that she would be leaving for Cardiff in ten days' time, she accepted the news without flinching.

THIRTEEN

When Josi saw his son coming towards his house, he was full of anger. Pride, which he didn't know he possessed, churned up inside him; he was ashamed that Tom should see his poor cottage, clean now, but badly in need of paint and wallpaper, bare of furniture, short of every comfort.

He went out on to the path as though to forbid him to enter.

'Father, I'm sorry,' Tom said, his voice so meek and troubled that Josi was immediately placated. Whatever Tom wanted, it wasn't to humble him.

'Come in, son.'

Josi put his arm round Miriam's shoulders when he went back to the kitchen, a gesture both acknowledging and supporting her.

'Here's Tom come,' he said.

Miriam and Tom managed to smile at each other. The three stood together, formally, awkwardly, the evening sun slanting in at them through the open door. Tom's dark suit, his white shirt with its stiff high collar, added to the gulf between them; Josi was in his shirt sleeves, a brown spotted handkerchief at his neck, Miriam in a print dress, a long blue and white apron over it

'It's a fine evening,' Josi said. He smiled, encouraging Tom to give them his message.

'I must fetch some things from the line,' Miriam said.

'No, don't go. I want you to hear what I've got to say.' Tom turned back to his father. 'Yes, it's bad news, I'm afraid. Doctor Andrews says that Mother is dying. He doesn't think she'll last till Michaelmas; he's sure she can't live beyond Christmas. I wondered if you could possibly see your way to coming home for these last weeks.'

The shock in his father's eyes halted him for a moment but he steeled himself to finish. 'I know I'm making difficulties for you in asking; I know that. All the same, I don't know what to do but ask. It's all she wants. She talks of it all the time. And she's dying.'

Josi sat down heavily in the armchair. Tom saw how he would look as an old man; shrunken and defeated.

Miriam caught a sob in her throat, made one strange, child-like sound, then was silent again.

'Make us a cup of tea, love,' Josi said at last. He got up and squeezed her arm. His words were for her. 'It's like a bad dream, isn't it?' They stood together for a moment.

Then Miriam went to the pump to fill the kettle and Josi put some sticks on the fire.

'Sit down, man,' he said to his son. 'We don't charge for sitting. How did you come, then?'

'On the train from Llanfryn to Newcastle, a taxi-cab from there; walked from the main road because the driver was afraid of the hill.'

'Thought I hadn't heard a horse.'

Miriam put the kettle on the fire and got out cups and saucers. They had had their supper; she wondered what she could offer Tom; there was sanity in thinking about food and drink. She gripped the table as she caught Josi's eyes upon her, so full of love and pain they seemed.

'Will you have some bacon?' she asked Tom.

'I've eaten, thank you. In The Swan. I had to wait for the taxi-cab to come back from Aberaeron; someone going to the seaside earlier on.'

For a time no one spoke. The fire hissed and spat; it was a long time before the kettle started to hum.

'Does *she* know?' Josi asked, then.

'No. Neither does Catrin. Doctor Andrews told me so that I'd agree to letting Catrin go away. He doesn't want her at home.'

'Cancer, I suppose?'

'I didn't ask. He had a specialist some time back, he said.'

'Yes. He told me it was to do with the headaches she'd been having.'

'It wasn't that.'

'No.'

'Here's your cup of tea, at last.' Miriam's hand shook as she passed it to him. The cup clattered in the saucer.

'You'll have to stay the night,' Josi said. 'You can have a blanket on the floor down here.'

'Thank you. I could walk back to The Swan but it's a fair step; I'd rather do it in the morning.'

'What time is your train?'

'Nine o'clock.'

'You'll need to start at seven, then.'

'Half past six, seven.'

'How was the hay?'

'Very good – same here I suppose?'

'Aye. Pretty fair.'

'Davy is forecasting a wet August, though.'

'Always does, man. Prophet of doom, old Davy. Take no notice It'll be a good harvest, the barley's tinkling already.'

Miriam went back to the table where she'd been ironing. She started folding little garments and putting them to air on the brass rail over the fire.

Tom knew they wouldn't talk again about his mother until the morning. In the morning, his father would tell him what he had decided. He had to wait till then.

It was strange how he could sit so comfortably in the same room as his father's mistress. She didn't look like anyone's mistress; just an ordinary, pretty woman, brown and freckled. Or was there something about her eyes? Strange eyes, wild and frightened, a strange colour, almost gold.

'I'll go up, then,' Miriam told Josi. She looked a second at Tom, but didn't smile.

'Bring her down after you've fed her,' Josi said. 'She likes it by the fire.'

'You can fetch her down.'

'I'm not going back to Oxford,' Tom said, when Miriam had left, shutting the door behind her.

'Quite right.'

'Catrin's going to Cardiff to train as a nurse – that's the latest. I've no idea what made her change her mind. She doesn't say. Art School one week, nursing the next; sudden as that. Doctor Andrews pulled a few strings and got her in to the Infirmary in Cardiff. The course started in May, but he knew somebody.'

'Does *she* know that Catrin's going?'

'Yes.'

'Sure you won't have a bite to eat? What about some oat-cakes and buttermilk?'

'I'll have a couple of oat-cakes then, and another cup of tea.'

'Listen to that bird. Blackbirds sing differently up here; same notes, different tunes.'

'I knew a blackbird could whistle The Old Hundredth.'

'No doubt.'

'Heard it four or five times.'

'You drink too much, boy, I tell you all the time. The Old Hundredth!'

They continued to mutter at each other good-naturedly for a while; talking of anything except what was in both their minds.

'What's the work like, up here?'

'Work's much the same everywhere, isn't it. It's a hard place, though, if you live in. The food's terrible.'

'Can't be worse than we used to have at school. We had a dish called Workhouse Special. No one could eat it and we were all starving.'

'Starving? You don't know the meaning of the word, you and your school. When I was seven or eight I used to work for my Uncle Dan on a Saturday morning. Collecting acorns for the pigs, something like that. Hard work too, scrabbling under the wet leaves; you'd work for an hour to get a bucketful. And do you know what my wages were after a morning's work? Four hours' work?'

'I used to dream about food in that school. Liver and onions. Dumplings.'

They were silent at last, the gathering darkness gave them the courage to be silent and to look at each other.

He despises me, Josi thought, I don't blame him. When he's older, perhaps he'll be kinder, more understanding.

I think he should come home, Tom thought, it's his duty to come home. He shouldn't have left Mother. All the same.... All the same....

Each wondered what decision would have been reached by morning.

At last Josi yawned and bent to loosen his bootlaces.

'I'll have a bit of a walk while there's still some light,' Tom said, realizing that he'd be in the way while they were getting ready for bed.

117

'See you in the morning then, son. I'll be down by half past five. You'll have the fire going and the kettle boiling by then, no doubt.'

'What shall I do, sweetheart? Tell me.'

Miriam didn't answer. She knew he would go back to his wife. He was a good man, kind and dutiful. It was only because of the baby that he'd ever been able to leave in the first place.

She found his hand and kissed it.

'It'll only be for a short time,' he said. 'I think I'll have to go back. What do you say? Oh, Miriam, say something. Please.'

She sat up in bed and looked towards the window. It was utterly dark, as dark outside as in.

'There isn't a choice,' she said at last. 'You must go.' She felt his body slacken with relief.

'It'll be so difficult, though, won't it. Seeing her growing weaker, trying to be patient. We shouldn't talk about afterwards, I know, but we'll be able to get married afterwards. Won't we? Miriam?'

'Perhaps so.'

'Why perhaps? What can stop us? Afterwards? Miriam?'

But she had no more comfort for him. It suddenly seemed monstrous, what he intended to do. How could he leave her now? How could he?

'Why should I want to marry you? What's so wonderful about marriage? Christian marriage ordained for the procreation of children. Only that? It's a denigration of love, it seems to me. Animals mate to procreate the species; human love is a different thing, surely, something larger – it's got to be – an explanation of life, its health, the only thing that makes it bearable. I don't want Christian wedlock. I don't want to be locked to anyone, not even to you, and I'm not a Christian, I keep telling you that. I'm not a Christian.'

'Never mind, never mind. I'll have you as you are, freckles and all and thin as a whippet. Lie down, my little one. My little pagan.'

Josi's voice was low and his hands tender and soothing, but she seemed in a fever.

'I can't lie down. I'm going outside. I can't stay in bed. It's too hot up here. There's no air. Just over the stile the grass is cropped like moss, it'll be soft and cold. Won't you come out with me, Josi? Let's pretend this hasn't happened. The moon will be up soon. I want you, Josi, and I won't have you long. You'll go before the end of the week, I know, and I'll be half mad for you. Walking round in my flannel petticoat and singing like old Marged Rhys.'

'Lie down now, there's a good girl.' Josi's voice was the one he had for a frightened animal. 'Lie down now.'

'I'm going alone, then. If you won't come with me, I'm going alone.'

She sprang up from bed and almost made the door, but Josi was too quick for her. He was too strong for her; he picked her up, carried her back and laid her on the bed.

'A hussy, that's what you are, a shameless hussy. Can't live decently between four walls. No. And you're proud of it, aren't you. Proud of being a man's downfall. Proud of being a man's whore.'

But she, having heard his monologue many times before, wasn't attending to a word of it, only kissing him and crying and keeping up a monologue of her own, 'Open up, oh ye gates, for the king of glory to come in. My beloved put in his hand by the hole of the door, and my bowels were moved for him.'

They found peace and oblivion at last. That one night more.

In the morning, Josi told his son that he would be returning to Hendre Ddu before the end of the week.

'It'll serve Isaac Lloyd right, that's one thing I'm glad about,' Miriam said. 'The old fox. Only why should I call him a fox, a fox may be sly but he has his dignity and a sense of fair play; Isaac Lloyd has neither; he's a twisted old miser and I'm glad you'll be out of his clutches.'

'I'll have Prince and Mabon and the wagon here by day-break on Friday,' Tom said. 'We'll load up; take every stick of yours with us. We'll leave it all at Garnant Mill, they've got any amount of room. I can say it's stuff I had at Oxford; they know I'm leaving.'

It's all too easy, Miriam thought, swinging from one mood to another. It's our little home which is being disposed of, it's not just furniture. It's too easy. Too easy.

Tom suggested getting lodgings for Miriam and the baby in Carmarthen, but Miriam had seen a vacant room advertised in Morfa, the seaside village they could see from the top of the hill, and was determined that that was where she would stay.

Tom brought out a leather purse from his pocket.

'Pay three months' rent in advance,' he told Miriam. 'Pay whatever they ask. Don't stint yourself in anything.'

'I've got money,' Miriam said, 'I shall be quite all right.'

Tom, realizing at once how tactless he had been, looked apologetically at his father. But Josi was smiling and looking at Miriam so tenderly that Tom couldn't wait to be away.

'Don't hate me,' he said quietly to Miriam as he left. 'Please don't hate me.' He was afraid to offer her his hand.

'I must go too,' Josi said after his son had left. 'I must go to work.' But he didn't go. He sat down again in the armchair by the fire and took Miriam on his knee and when she cried, he cried, and they sat without a word, their tears mingling.

The baby was unsettled; crying even after Miriam had fed her, crying through the morning. I'm losing my milk, Miriam thought, whatever happens I mustn't lose my milk. She didn't ask to be born. Oh, Elen, smile at me.

In a panic, she drank almost a pint of buttermilk straight from the pitcher, then went out to sit on the doorstep in the sun and tried to will herself to think about anything other than Josi; their parting. She tried to think about milk, a land flowing with milk and honey, about water, about the pool in the river where she had swum as a child, how green and cold it was, dappled by shafts of sunlight breaking through the high elms. You could see fish darting about under the water. When she was about seven, she had won first prize for a composition about fishing, though she had never caught a fish or tried to catch a fish in her life, and Owen Brynglas, a famous fisherman, aged nine, had thrown a stone after her. Rain. That was another beautiful sight, rain, falling straight and silent on the land, possessing it. Rain. Once, it had rained so hard that her bed was soaked through in the night. She had had to sleep with her mother, then, and had discovered that she only had one blanket on the bed. After that they had always slept together in the driest part of the room, with three blankets. Rain. Rain. He shall come down like rain upon the mown grass; as showers that water the earth. The story of Noah; how moving. When the dove had brought back the green leaf. And God's rainbow over the world. 'And the Lord said in his heart, I will not again curse the ground any more for man's sake; for the imagination of man's heart is evil from his youth; neither will I again smite any more every thing living, as I have done. While the earth remaineth, seed-time and harvest and cold and heat and summer and winter, and day and night shall not cease.' That's it. That's all there is. Man is weak, imperfect, irredeemable, yet summer and winter and day and night shall not cease. That's as much religion as I need. That's enough for me. Who needs more?

Feeling calmer, Miriam fetched the baby and put her to the breast again, but again she rejected the offered nipple, turning her face away and crying as before.

Miriam, who had tried being calm and still, now felt compelled to action. She wrapped the baby in a light, carrying shawl and walked hurriedly down the steep hill to the village. She was in her ordinary working dress, a pale grey calico which she used to wear to school during fine weather – it was shabby now and stained – she was far from looking her best and she felt tired and dishevelled. In spite of it, she decided that she would call at the white-washed cottage near the beach, where she'd seen the vacancy advertised. The sooner she was settled in somewhere the better. It was her fault that the baby was upset.

It was the beginning of August, another cloudless day, but there was no one on the narrow shingle beach. The pale sea frilled on to the grey and white stones, seagulls bobbed on the gentle waves like ducks on a pond, the only sound was the soft splash of the incoming tide. It was a new world. She let the breath and pulse of it comfort her for a few moments.

Then her restlessness returned; she turned away from the sea and walked to the cottage.

She tapped at the open door. The slate-roofed, four-roomed cottage was the type she knew very well; they were everywhere in West Wales, only the smooth white stones decorating the front garden instead of flowers were different, and the shells arranged and set in intricate patterns around the door. The smell was different, too; seaweed and tarred driftwood instead of the familiar smell of chickens and cows.

'I've come about the accommodation,' she said. An elderly woman was suddenly before her.

'Come inside, please.'

She was shown into the kitchen which was bright and pretty; scarlet geraniums on the window-sill, a green chenille cloth on the table, a gleaming range, brass ornaments.

'What a nice kitchen,' she said.

'What is it you're wanting?'

'Whatever you've got.'

'Is it for a holiday?'

'No, for longer than that. For some months at least.'

'Just the two of you and the baby?'

'I'm on my own. Just myself and the baby.'

'What I usually have is people on holiday. I had a honeymoon couple last month. From the South. Merthyr.'

'I could pay whatever you charge.'

'It isn't that exactly, is it?'

'What is it, then?'

'There'd be talk. A woman alone with a baby makes talk in these parts. Would your husband be coming now and then?'

'I'm not married.'

'Sit down there a minute.'

Miriam sat where she was told and looked at the woman; thin, bird-like, dressed in black with a black handkerchief over her hair, her expression neither kind or unkind.

'Did he take advantage of you?'

Miriam realized that the woman wanted an excuse to take pity on her, but she wasn't the type to ask or even allow favours.

'No,' she said. 'It wasn't like that.'

'Haven't you a home?'

'My mother's dead. I did have a house of my own, but it was a school house and of course I had to leave as soon as I knew about the baby.'

'You were a schoolmistress, were you?'

'A very small school. Twenty-three children.'

'Where was this?'

'In Carmarthenshire. Rhydfelen, Carmarthenshire.'

The baby, who had been comforted to sleep during the walk, woke again and started to cry. Miriam tightened the shawl around her and stood up.

'I'll go, then,' she said.

'What will you do?'

'I'll have to start telling lies, I suppose. Buy a wedding ring. Say I'm a widow.'

'It'll be easier to get lodgings in a town.'

'I don't like living in a town. Well, I may have to.'

'Is it a boy or a girl?'

'A girl.'

'How old is she?'

'Ten weeks.'

'You're welcome to sit and feed her.'

'She doesn't seem very well today. She doesn't usually cry like this.'

Miriam sat again, feeling exhausted and dispirited. She took Mari-Elen out of the shawl and laid her across her lap. She could feel her little knees drawing up sharply, as though she was in pain.

'They bring their love with them,' the older woman said.

'And their care.'

'Yes.'

'They say a woman is in her care when she's carrying, but believe me, she's in her care as long as they're both alive.'

'You have children, then?'

'Three sons.'

'Living nearby?'

'No. In London. The eldest bought a dairy in St John's Wood in London when his father died, and the others went up to join him. I never see them. Only the care I have now. I wonder if she'd take water from a spoon? There's a drop in the kettle will soon cool.'

She brought Miriam some water, still slightly warm, and Miriam gave the baby a spoonful. She gulped and spluttered and then cried with even greater ferocity.

'Let me have her.'

The woman took the baby and wrapped her very tightly in the shawl so that she couldn't move her arms or legs. Then, tilting her slightly, she managed to get her to take a little of the water; three or four teaspoonfuls. Then she held her to her face and recited an old rhyme to her and then another. Soon the baby's crying slackened and after a few minutes she was quiet,

'Thank you,' Miriam said. Once more she got up.

'What you should do is get someone to foster her for you. Then you could get work.'

'No, I won't do that.'

'I don't mean have her adopted; she'd still be yours.'

'I'd rather keep her with me.'

'How will you live? Will her father send money?'

Miriam didn't answer. She held out her arms for the baby.

'You'd better stay here, I suppose,' the woman said.

'If it suits you.'

'It will have to, I suppose. When do you want to come?'

'Tomorrow evening.'

'Five shillings a week, I charge.'

Miriam took out a sovereign from a purse in her pocket. She had five left; the last of the money she had managed to save while she was teaching. When that was finished she would really be a kept woman.

'Would you like to see the bedroom and the parlour?'

'No, thank you. I know it will suit me. Also, I won't want to use the parlour unless you'd rather keep me out of the kitchen.'

'Live as family, four and sixpence,' the woman said.

She passed Miriam the baby, now fast asleep, and got her purse from the dresser drawer. She put the sovereign into it and handed Miriam a florin.

'I'm Mrs Thomas,' she said, 'Lily Thomas. Widow.'

FOURTEEN

Catrin withdrew from the day-to-day life of the farm. Everyone thought she was busy with preparations for her departure to Cardiff; in fact she spent her time in her room, studying herself in the mirror for hours, doing absolutely nothing.

In making her decision to train as a nurse, she had thought she was taking a step which would radically change her life and was realizing that it had in no way changed her. She had expected immediate metamorphosis into a completely different being, selfless, whereas she was still, she knew it, the immature, over-emotional girl thwarted in her first love encounter. The big gesture seemed to have been in vain, even rather silly.

Doctor Andrews, because he was a little in love with her, had some idea of what she was going through, and on his daily visits to her mother never failed to spend five minutes with her, talking about the more exciting aspects of modern medicine; the advances being made in operation techniques, the newest theories about nervous diseases. Realizing that she was intent on sacrificing herself, he wanted her at least to consider the sacrifice worthwhile.

In the event, it wasn't the doctor's pep talks which strengthened her resolve, but something else entirely.

On 5 August, a few days before she was due to leave home, it was announced in the papers that England had declared war on Germany.

From her earliest schooldays, a war between the great powers, England, France and Germany, had been prophesied; the inevitable outcome of their increasing military strength and continual jockeying for position. Now that the war had come, it seemed the appropriate time for putting aside personal vanities like love affairs and painting and drawing, and for making a serious commitment. It wasn't so much patriotism that moved her as a foreboding of difficult times ahead, a foreboding that life was earnest and might be grim. The outbreak of war enabled her to forget herself and really think of herself as a nurse.

It was the following day that Josi returned home. He walked about the farm in his old way, talking to everyone, taking it easy, so entirely master of the situation that there was little speculation about why he'd come back; he was there, that was enough. Everyone was pleased.

It was only with Rachel that his composure left him; she had changed so much in his absence, had lost such a great deal of weight; lost her hold on life, it seemed.

'Rachel,' he said. 'I'm sorry to see you so low.'

'Did Tom ask you to come back? Was that why you came?' She struggled to sit up, not noticing his shocked expression or his faltering tones.

'That mostly. Other things as well.'

'We're man and wife, Josi,' she said.

He took her hand. Her wedding ring was loose on her finger.

'We are, Rachel.'

'This is where you should be.'

'It is.'

'Don't leave me again. There's no need for it.'

'I won't leave you again. Believe me I won't. I'm sorry to have caused you such distress. I'll be here from now on.'

With that she had to be satisfied. She was satisfied. Rachel believed her husband had returned because he had received assurances of her forgiveness. Her heart grew large with forgiveness; it seemed the sweetest thing in the world.

She called Tom up to her room when Josi had gone downstairs and told him to arrange weekly payments for the baby until her sixteenth birthday. Tom promised to see the solicitor that afternoon.

'I want the payments to continue, remember, even if I should die.'

'Of course they shall, Mam, of course. I think you're acting generously and properly.'

Tom bent and kissed his mother's forehead. He was relieved that she hadn't asked him any embarrassing questions; whether he had seen Miss Lewis and the baby, where they and his father had been living. He considered his mother a perfect lady.

'Now that Father is home, I think I'll apply for a commission with the Monmouthshire Regiment. I was in the Officers Training

Corps at school, so I don't think they'd turn me down. I feel I ought to go. It seems my duty. They say it will be all over by Christmas.'

'Tom, but you're needed here.'

'Not now. Not now that Father is back.'

'Tom. Oh Tom, I suppose you must do what you think is right.'

'I think it's right. Germany has marched into Belgium, a peaceful little country, not much bigger than Wales; that seems indefensible. The English and French armies will have to put a stop to that, it seems to me. Don't you think so?'

'So I'm going to lose you and Catrin?'

'You won't lose either of us. We'll come back when it's all over and you'll be proud of us. I'm very pleased now that Catrin is going to be a nurse; it's the very thing I'd want her to do. After her training, she can volunteer to nurse the wounded.'

'But you said it would be over by Christmas.'

'The newspapers could be wrong, I suppose.'

Josi read the accounts of war, but couldn't concentrate on them. Things outside his control didn't occupy his mind. Miriam occupied his mind. Was he right to have left her? Rachel was dying, that was obvious even to him, yet she seemed the stronger of the two women. It wasn't that Miriam had wept or clung to him; quite the reverse. When he had got back to their little cottage a couple of days ago, she had seemed terribly and awfully composed, drawing away from him when he'd tried to touch her, as animals do when injured.

'I've found lodgings for her and me, Jos, in that cottage I told you about. I know you won't be able to visit us, I won't expect it, but perhaps you'll write a line or two now and again. Care of Mrs Thomas, Carreg Las, Morfa. I expect you'll change, though, Josi, people change when someone is dying, death turns even the best people into hypocrites. You'll become religious, you shall see; more religious, I mean. You'll think of me as your fall from grace and you'll pray for deliverance from the sins of the flesh. Yes, you will, Josi. Never mind, I won't change. You can be sure of me.'

'Don't torture me, girl. You know how I love you. Don't break my heart with your nonsense. I don't know how I can bring myself to leave you, home is where you are, you know that, Miriam. Only a little month we've had together here, and we thought we'd never be parted again. What can I do to show you how much I love you?'

If Miriam had asked him to stay, he would have stayed, he knew it. But she didn't. Only tormented him in the way she had, so that there was only one way of release, and that way, she denied him.

They had spent the entire night in feverish thrust and parry, she never relenting, always keeping him away, beating him with her hard little fists whenever he tried to touch her. And at dawn they were still awake. Still alone and separate, they heard the first bird piping up. Then another and another, thrushes and blackbirds, robins and linnets, reaching an urgent, tumultuous crescendo.

'They really seem to think it's wonderful, don't they; being alive,' Miriam said, her voice calm. 'Listen to them straining their little throats. It's only another day, you foolish creatures, it's not the blessed resurrection.'

'Let them be,' Josi said. He put his hand out to touch her and found her small and quiet. She didn't resist when he lifted her towards him.

'You're my new day, Josi,' she said afterwards. In the faint light of dawn they clung together and kissed in absolute surrender. They half-slept, kissed as they slept, clung together in their despair.

That evening after dark, he took her and the baby to their new home in Morfa. Mrs Thomas came to the door at Miriam's first tap. She seemed surprised to see a man with her, perhaps relieved, but didn't ask him in. 'Goodbye,' Miriam said, touching his hand briefly and following Mrs Thomas into the lamp-lit kitchen. 'Goodbye, my girl.'

The tearing pain of parting remained with him still. So many songs he had sung about heartache, but they were all inadequate. Words turned about and stuck in his throat. Only the wind on the moor and the rain and the eerie broken cry of the curlews seemed to express the pain he felt.

She had shed a radiance on his life, he had never understood it, only accepted it. She made him feel as previously he had never felt for a woman, had felt only for an occasional frosty night when the stars shone on the hard, bright snow, at a funeral when the choir of men's voices seemed to touch the nerve at the centre of existence. She affected him like stars and music. How could he do without her? He walked about the farm feeling like the husk of the man he was.

★

Tom hadn't told Catrin that their father was returning. She walked into the kitchen at midday and found him there talking to Miss Rees. For a moment she neither moved nor spoke, so great was her shock at seeing him; her heart pounded and her mouth was dry.

'What's up with you?' Josi asked her, and to her surprise she found herself crying in his arms as she had done when she was a child, as though he was the only one who could help her. And he patted her back and waited for her to stop.

'Have you heard about the war?' she asked at last. She hoped her emotional outburst would be ascribed to that cause.

'Yes, I've seen the papers. Yesterday's and today's.'

'Have you heard that I'm going nursing?'

'Yes, I've heard that, too.'

'Will you be here while I'm away?'

'Yes, I'll be here.'

He was so calm and self-assured, seemed so strong and dependable. Yet, he had left her mother for another woman; Catrin realized that she shouldn't be basking in the warmth of his presence. He couldn't help himself, she thought, any more than I could help falling in love with Edward Turncliffe. Nothing – she knew it – could keep her from Edward, neither family nor career nor the knowledge of hurting Rose whom she had liked and admired. She was no different. No better. Perhaps no one was. She had been too young and green to understand. She patted her father's arm, forgiving him.

He thought her touch seemed like an appeal for help.

'Don't let them get you down,' he said.

'Who do you mean?'

'Anybody.'

He thought of Isaac Lloyd, his boss for the last six weeks. How had the man become such a tyrant? How had it happened? What had twisted his nature? So that he had a need to antagonize every man and woman on his farm. Why? 'The men will work twice as hard if you send them a good tea and give them time to eat it.' 'When I want advice from you I'll ask for it.' Every move Josi had made to try to humanize conditions had been countered by greater severity. When Josi had told him he was leaving, Lloyd had treated the statement with scorn. 'You'll leave when I kick you out.' With no money and no reference, how could a workman leave? He was as tied as during the years of serfdom.

When Josi had told the farm lads of his departure, they had got up before dawn to help him load his furniture on to the wagon; partly, they liked him, mainly it was their delight that Isaac Lloyd was to be done down, to the best of their knowledge it was the first time such a thing had ever happened.

He wished he could warn Catrin about the Isaac Lloyds of the world, by all accounts there were plenty in the nursing profession. But she was young and resilient, and doubtless more charitable and understanding than he was.

'Be happy,' he said. 'Try to be happy.'

'I can't be happy so I'll have to be good, won't I?'

Josi wondered what she meant, but she smiled and drew herself away from him as though unwilling to be questioned.

He let her go, his thoughts returning to Miriam. It was worse for her than for him. He was in the bosom of his affectionate family and surrounded by old friends; she was alone with strangers. Would anyone comfort and help her when the baby was fretful in the night? She was more sensitive than it was possible to be, happier than anyone else in the world when she was happy, but easily cast down, easily frightened, easily hurt. If only she had been willing to come back to Llanfryn, to old Hetty. 'I won't go where you'll be tempted to visit me,' she had said, 'I know that would be worse for you.' She was brave and wise; all the same he wished she was at Llanfryn with her aunt.

Lowri came in from the yard and stood before him. She came from the same small hamlet as he did, they were distantly related.

She didn't say a word in greeting, just stood there looking at him with a familiar homely tenderness in her eyes. She reminded him of the picture of his mother as a child. He tried to think of something to say to her.

'It's whinberry tart today,' she said at last. 'Sali and I picked a basketful last night.'

'That's what I came home for,' Josi said.

They smiled at each other.

Tom wrote to Edward telling him that he intended applying for a commission. 'In a way I'm only escaping from the nightmare situation at home,' he wrote. 'Doctor Andrews has arranged for Catrin to be away so that she doesn't have to see Mother suffering – he says she will soon be much worse – but in fact it is I who would find it intolerable. Catrin is much harder, or much braver, than I am. So I shall go to Monmouth tomorrow and with any luck shall be in France within the month. I persuaded Father to come home, so I shall be leaving the farm in good hands.'

The next day he received a letter from Edward.

> Patriotism has filled my soul. I feel that nothing can be as worthwhile as a soldier's life, a soldier's death. I feel I have met my destiny. I have only one wish; to be leading a platoon in France and to be worthy of my country. You'll be glad to know that Rose and I were married quietly at the end of last month. Luckily she feels exactly as I do about everything. Please give my kindest regards to your beautiful sister.

Tom read the letter with awe, feeling ashamed of his far less elevated motives for joining the army.

'Edward sends you his regards,' he told Catrin over breakfast. 'He and Rose got married last month. Do you think you could find time to buy them a wedding present?'

'I think so. I'm going into Llanfryn with Doctor Andrews later on. What sort of thing would be suitable?'

'Ask Mother. She'll know.'

Catrin went upstairs shivering in the summer heat. Definite news at last, and she was glad of it. Now she would no longer be troubled by improbable dreams that he might still be remembering her from time to time. He was married. She had certain knowledge of it. Pain struck like a knife between her eyes.

She stood before the window of her bedroom and let the pain seep into her, nerve by nerve, cell by cell. She walked over to the mirror above her dressing-table to examine the pain. To her surprise it hadn't altered her appearance, the devastation was only inward. How could her silly face look so composed still? It seemed wrong.

She picked up her heavy silver hairbrush and struck the mirror, and for a second, while it cracked and splintered, she saw herself smashing into fragments. She screamed in terror, and when Nano rushed into the room she was just in time to save her from collapsing on to the floor.

'Whatever is it? Whatever is the matter? What have you done, you naughty girl?'

She dragged Catrin to the bed and managed to lift her on to it.

'Seven years' bad luck you've brought us. How did you manage it, you naughty girl? Thing are bad enough here as it is. What have you done?'

When Doctor Andrews arrived, Miss Rees took him first into Catrin's room. She was thoroughly alarmed at the way she was lying on the bed absolutely still.

'Now what is it?' the doctor asked the girl after dismissing Miss Rees. Her pulse was normal. She was breathing evenly.

'I haven't much time. Tell me what it is. Have you changed your mind about leaving home?'

'No.'

'Then what is it? You can't just lie here all the morning like Sleeping Beauty. I thought you were coming into Llanfryn with me. What is it?'

He took her hand to pull her into a sitting position, and to his surprise she squeezed his hand and looked at him piteously, her eyes brimming over with tears.

He pulled his hand away. 'I must go to your mother. I'll expect you in the car in ten minutes.'

He strode in to Mrs Evans's room. Could the girl be in love with him? Was she trying to draw attention to herself? Angling for him? The possibility swam in his head like whisky on an empty stomach.

'Mrs Evans,' he said as he entered the room, abrupt in his excitement, 'may I have your permission to ask your daughter to marry me?'

He hadn't meant to say it, had resolved against it time after time, but the pressure on his hand, that look of hers had confounded him.

'Indeed you may,' Rachel Evans said, looking very happy. 'Indeed you may. And I shall hope for your success.'

While he examined Mrs Evans, Miss Rees, who had been in the adjoining dressing-room hurried downstairs to find Tom.

'Mr Tom,' she said. 'I think you had a letter from Mr Turncliffe this morning.'

'Yes I did, Nano.'

'Will you be writing back to him today?'

'I wrote to him yesterday – our letters crossed – but I'll be writing again in a day or two, I think.'

'Tell him that Miss Rees has got some very special news for him and that she hopes he'll come back very quickly to hear it.'

'He won't be coming back this summer I'm afraid, Nano.'

'Won't he? Are you sure?'

'Quite sure. Would you like to write to him yourself? I can give you his address. He'd like to hear from you.'

'No, I won't write to him. Perhaps you can give him a message from me. Tell him that the doctor is going to beat him to it unless he gets in touch with us very soon.'

'Unless he gets in touch with us very soon? What can that mean? I don't think he'll make head nor tail of that message, Nano.'

'Oh yes he will. You just tell him what I said; he'll make head or tail of it, indeed he will.'

'The doctor is going to beat him to it if he...'

'That's right.'

'Could this be something to do with Catrin?'

'It could. Yes, it could be something to do with Miss Catrin.'

'Oh Nano, you've got quite the wrong idea. Mr Turncliffe got married last month, he was never interested in Catrin except as my sister.'

'Does Miss Catrin know that he got married last month?'

'Yes. I told her this morning. She's promised to buy him a...'

But Miss Rees had left him and in no time at all was with Catrin again, cradling her in her arms, calling her a white flower, a treasure, a skein of silk, her golden one.

FIFTEEN

Doctor Andrews called at Hendre Ddu that evening after supper and found an opportunity of speaking alone with Catrin. By this time his ardour had cooled a little and he felt rather grateful to her for turning him down. Her manner was so gentle; she seemed so pleased and flattered by his offer, and gave such excellent reasons for refusing it, that he left caring for her more deeply than when he arrived. Instead of injuring his self-esteem, she had managed to bolster it, seeming to suggest, though without saying so, that if he were to ask her again some time in the future, she might have changed her mind. He made her promise to write to him.

She left home at the end of the week as planned and was immediately plunged into the harsh realities of a nurse's life. From being a cosseted young lady, working when she felt like it, but more often pleasantly idle, she was for twelve hours a day at everyone's beck and call, given the meanest and dreariest tasks and forever told to look sharp about them. Everything was strange, the clanging noise and the cold, frightening smells of the wards, the food, dismal and inadequate, the cell-like room she shared with two other girls. For the first month, every muscle of her body ached, her eyes were red-rimmed and dull from the long hours, her feet so swollen that she couldn't lace her heavy shoes. A probationer nurse, it seemed to her, worked as hard as any man at the harvest, as hard as a horse hauling timber, as hard as the wife of a smallholding whose labours were endless and proverbial. She was too exhausted to think about Edward except in the few moments it took her to drop off to sleep every night. She was far less miserable than she had been at home. She didn't for a moment regret her decision to leave; she was certain that she had found her vocation.

At the end of the month, the Matron told her that she was pleased with her progress, that she had already – in practical nursing – caught up with the other probationers who had been at the Infirmary since May, and that she would now be given an easier duty rota, so that she could find time to study for the preliminary examination which was being held in three weeks' time.

'If you pass the prelim, you can ask for a transfer to a military hospital,' one of her colleagues whispered to her over the sluices one morning. 'They're crying out for nurses for the soldiers coming back from France. It can't be worse than this and it might be better.'

'My brother's in the army,' Catrin had whispered back. 'All the same, I think I'll finish my training.'

Within a fortnight of the outbreak of war, Tom had succeeded in obtaining a commission. Kitchener, who had been made Secretary of War, was determined to raise, train and equip new armies of unprecedented size almost overnight, and the newspapers, lashing up a frenzy of patriotism by the tales of atrocities perpetrated on the innocent Belgians, ensured that there was no shortage of volunteers. Indeed they flowed in at a rate which put a heavy strain on the machinery for accommodating and training them. Tom spent a hectic but enjoyable six weeks, teaching the newest recruits to march and handle a rifle. It was an out-door life with plenty of congenial company and high spirits. Morale was high; everyone seeming eager to get out to France before it was all over. The newspapers published only favourable news, and though there were rumours in the officers' mess of retreats and set-backs and long casualty lists, it was considered bad form to discuss them.

After six weeks Tom was given leave. He didn't look forward to going home. During his weeks with the army he had managed to push his mother's illness to the back of his mind; he was both reluctant to have to face it again and ashamed of his reluctance.

It was a Sunday evening when he arrived home. The harvest had been gathered in and the men and maids were at evening service.

Only Miss Rees came to the door to welcome him, and she without any of her usual vivacity, her face old and unsmiling.

'Is Mother worse?' he asked her.

'Much worse.'

'She, who was usually so stubbornly optimistic about everything, seemed to have learned resignation.

'Much worse. Don't go up to her till you've had a bite to eat.

135

You'll be very upset. You father is up with her now. He's very good, sits with her for hours; as soon as he gets in from the fields at night.'

'Do you think we should get Catrin home?'

'No, not yet. It's not necessary. Lowri is doing the night nursing and she's a good quiet girl, she doesn't agitate your poor mother. I think your poor mother would be agitated to have a proper nurse, though we may have to have one soon, we leave it to Doctor Andrews. It's to be as he says. He's like an angel from heaven and may God forgive me for thinking him not good enough for Miss Catrin. My dearest wish now is to see them married. I tell Mrs Evans, "Mrs Evans bach, Miss Catrin is going to have the best husband any girl ever had and better, and she deserves it too, little silk, for who is she but the best, and the daughter of the best woman ever trod the earth".'

Miss Rees talked on as she cut bread and butter and carved meat and prepared a salad. Her words were as fluent as ever but their tone was different. Previously there was always a perilously high note in her voice, it was only a breath away from laughter, now it was flat and joyless.

Tom ate his supper, his first proper meal for twenty-four hours, watched over by the old woman.

'You've put on weight, my boy. Your poor mother will be happy to see you looking so well.'

'I've put on a stone in six weeks.'

'It's a grand life, then, is it?'

'It's a healthy life, I suppose. I'm out of doors all day. The food's not marvellous but there's plenty of it.'

'Have you come across Jim Brynteg yet?'

'No, I haven't. Is he with the Monmouthshire Regiment?'

'He's with the army, anyhow, and I told his mother you'd look out for him. She's very worried about him, because as you know poor Jim was never very....' Miss Rees tapped her forehead.

'Several boys have gone from these parts, and more will go now that the harvest is in. I don't know who will run the farms, I'm sure. There's no guarantee that they'll be home for the ploughing, is there?'

'No indeed, no guarantee.'

'But Christmas you said, Mr Tom.'

'Christmas nineteen-eighteen perhaps, Christmas nineteen-twenty.'

'Don't let's have any of that gloom in front of your poor mother, now.'

'Of course not.'

'I've told her you'll be home for the ploughing, if not before.'

Tom had finished his meal and was wondering if he could smoke for five minutes before going upstairs to his mother. He brought out his pipe and pouch of tobacco and laid them on the table in front of him. In a low, expressionless voice he started to recite:

> *I heard the crane cry unto men his greeting,*
> *To tell them it was time to drive the plough,*
> *Ah, friend, he set my sorry heart a-beating*
> *For others have my fertile acres now.*

There was a moment's silence.

'That's a very sad verse, Mr Tom. Who wrote that sad verse, I'd like to know?'

'A Greek poet, Nano, two or three thousand years ago.'

'Dear, dear. I thought that crane didn't sound like one of our birds, somehow, unless it was a *crehydd*; he's a grave old bird indeed. Well, there's no need for us to concern ourselves with those old Greeks, is there. And no one shall have your fertile acres, I can tell you that. Not while Miss Rees has any breath in her body.'

Nano's majestic chest rose and fell behind her starched white apron. Tom wondered whether he would ever see her again. He put down his pipe, still unlit.

'I've got something to show you, Nano.'

He pulled out a white envelope from the inside pocket of his army tunic. He passed her the photograph it held.

Miss Rees took it over to the lamp.

'Very nice,' she said at last. 'A very nice, pretty young lady. Who is she, Mr Tom?'

'Her name is May Malcolm. She's the step-daughter of my colonel. We've only met twice or three times but she's promised to write to me when I go to France. I promised to keep you informed, didn't I?'

'France is it, Mr Tom?'

'I think so. After I get back on Saturday.'

Nano's chest rose and fell again.

'Go up to see your poor mother now,' she said. 'Show her the photograph.'

Tom pushed his pipe back into his pocket and got to his feet.

'Is she church or chapel, say?' Miss Rees asked, as he reached the door.

'Heavens above, she's only promised to write to me, Nano.'

'A lot can happen in letters, remember. Perhaps she would be kind enough to send a few lines to your poor mother too. It would give her something to think about. A step-daughter of a colonel would be something to think about, wouldn't it. What is a colonel exactly? Very important, I know. Something like a Lord Lieutenant, I suppose. A wife changes with her husband anyway, so it doesn't matter too much. All the same, it would be nice if she was chapel.'

Tom was glad that Nano had warned him of his mother's condition. As it was, his heart seemed to contract with pity as he looked at her; she was wasted to a shadow. Looking at her face, he could see the skull beneath the skin. Your poor mother. He heard Nano's voice.

Her eyes lit up, though, to see him, and she grasped his hand with great strength. He forced himself to smile at her.

'How handsome you are, Tom,' she said. 'It's the first time I've seen you like your father. You've quite grown up.'

She turned her head towards Josi who was sitting by the window, as far as possible, perhaps, from the heat of the fire. He nodded at his son but didn't get up to greet him. 'Pity me, too,' he seemed to be saying. To Tom's dismay, tears started up in his eyes.

His mother, noticing, tried to make conversation. 'Tell us how they're treating you,' she said.

So he sat at her side and talked. He forced himself to talk. He told her about some of his brother-officers, about some of the men, tough young miners, many of them, with an original attitude to army regulations. He told her something about his colonel, intending to lead up to the pretty step-daughter, but by this time it was clear that she was too tired to listen to any more. 'Sleep now,' he said quietly, releasing his hand from hers; and she closed her eyes obediently and slept.

'I'll come down for a while,' Josi said. 'Nano shall come up for an hour or so.'

The two men left the room together, both on tip-toe.

'It's a mercy that they let you come home,' Josi said as they reached the sitting-room. 'Doctor Andrews is putting her on stronger drugs soon; he's warned us that she may not recognize us much after that. He doesn't think she'll last much longer now. She's in terrible pain from time to time, too much to bear, it seems, but she bears it. How long can you stay here?'

'I have to go back at the end of the week.'

'What then?'

'France probably.'

'Are you pleased?'

'No. Does that shock you?'

'Shock me? No. But I wish you were an idiot like the rest of them, it would be easier that way.'

'I suppose so. Turncliffe now. He can't wait to be on the front line. He thinks this war is the most glorious opportunity a young man ever had, the modern version of fighting the dragon; winning one's spurs. He thinks death for one's country is a privilege and an honour.'

'It's a good way to feel, if you can.'

'I can't.'

'Nor can I, indeed. That Turncliffe; I always thought him a bit fanciful.'

'Oh?'

'Talked a lot without saying much. You know what I mean.'

'I liked to hear him talk.'

'So did Catrin, I'm told.'

'What do you mean by that?'

Josi didn't answer. After all, what was the point in making trouble between friends? Poor little Catrin, though. Turncliffe had led her on, according to Nano. Pretty words; no more, perhaps. Young girls were too ready to fall in love. Wanted to kill herself, Nano said, when she knew he'd got married. Sadness everywhere. Everywhere.

They fell silent, listening to the ticking of the old clock.

'We need to talk about the farm,' Tom said, after a minute or two had ticked away.

'Yes, that's true.'

'It'll be mine, I suppose.'

'Yes. Her father's will.'

'You'll see to everything while I'm away?'

'Yes.'

'I thought you might live in Garth Ifan. You won't want to live here with...'

'With Miriam? No. But I can't go into that. It's impossible for me to think of any of that at the moment. I'll look after the farm. Just leave it at that.'

'I don't want to be morbid, Father, but what if I'm killed? What would happen then.'

'You've got time to make a will. Go to see Charles tomorrow. Only I don't want any of it, remember. Nothing but Cefn Hebog. Your mother wants me to have Cefn Hebog and that's right and proper. It should be mine. It was my grandfather's. Your great-grandfather, old Thomas Morgan...'

'Don't bring that up again, for God's sake. Cefn Hebog is yours. That's the one thing I'm sure of.'

'Good.'

'Who's living there now? Old Twm Price?'

'And his son.'

'They would move to Garth Ifan like a shot; it's a better farm, a much better house.'

'I know. But I don't want to plan anything now. It seems all wrong. I can't do it. I can't think of it.'

'All right. I won't mention it again.'

In bed that night, Tom couldn't sleep for thinking about his father and Miriam. He had a feeling that they would never live together again and felt the responsibility of having parted them. In a way, he'd been perfectly justified in telling his father of his mother's imminent death, but he couldn't discount his chief motive; that of abdicating his own responsibility; he had wanted to get away.

His mother would soon be dead, he felt rather as though she was already dead, and he feared what her death would do to his father, he seemed half-crazy with guilt.

There was the baby to think about. In six weeks with the army he had heard and thought so much about death. Twenty-five thousand Germans were said to have been killed in the last battle alone, and only a fool would believe that the English casualties could be as low as the newspapers pretended. Among so many deaths, a baby seemed important. What could he do? What could he say to his father?

He didn't see his father in the morning, he was already out when he got down. Lowri told him that his mother had had a fairly restful night and that Miss Rees wanted him to go upstairs after he'd had his breakfast.

Lowri's sister brought him breakfast. She was not yet fourteen, had only recently left school, and looked, in her blue, too-large dress and white apron, like a workhouse child. She told him her name was Megan.

'Are you happy here, Megan?'

'No, sir.'

Her answer took him aback so that he could think of nothing further to say. How could he expect her to be happy, he asked himself, as he ate his ham and eggs, in a house where the mistress was dying and no one had time to talk to her? Who was happy? He didn't look at her again, keeping his eyes on his paper. Her red hair and small red hands tormented him, though, for many days.

At first he thought his mother was already dead; she lay so flat and still and white on her bed.

'She'll wake soon,' Miss Rees whispered. 'And it's her best time. You'll really be able to talk to her.'

He sat at the bedside and looked at his mother's poor wasted body, her pale blue eyelids, her colourless lips.

As he looked at his mother, Miss Rees seemed to be studying him, as though she wanted to satisfy herself that his grief was sufficiently deep and tender. He wished for her sake that he could squeeze out a few tears. 'She's beautiful,' he said.

'Beautiful,' Miss Rees echoed. 'A saintly woman. Her soul is with God.'

'When does Doctor Andrews come?'

'About half past ten. You can stay until he comes.'

Two hours seemed like eternity. He wanted to walk over the fields and talk to the men.

'Being here upsets me too much,' he said, 'I'll come back later.'

As he stood up, his mother woke. 'Josi,' she said, her heart in her eyes.

'Mrs Evans bach, it's Mr Tom, look. Grown so big.'

'Tom. Yes of course it's Tom.'

She was too ill to hide her disappointment. She wanted only her husband.

'Have you shown your mother the picture of your young lady Mr Tom?'

'It's in my army tunic, I'm afraid.'

'Go and fetch it then, do, to show your mother.'

He went out obediently. 'The Colonel's step-daughter, if you please,' the old lady was saying. 'And a very pretty girl, too. He'll be bringing her to see you on his next holiday, you shall see.'

When he got back, Miss Rees had his mother propped up on pillows. She was chaffing her hands.

'What's her name?' his mother asked. 'She looks very nice. Pretty eyes.'

'May. May Malcom.'

'After the Queen, I expect,' Miss Rees said, 'May of Teck she was before she was married. Why didn't they call her Queen May? Such a nice name.'

'How old is she, Tom?'

Tom had no idea.

'Twenty-one,' Miss Rees said, 'six months younger than him. Just right.'

In a minute or two, his mother's voice and looks changed abruptly; the pain had come back. Miss Rees gave her some white powder in a glass of water, took away her pillows and sent Tom away.

SIXTEEN

'I have done no wickedness,' Miriam said aloud as she walked along the narrow tree-lined road with her baby.

'Such is the way of an adulterous woman, she eateth and wipeth her mouth and saith I have done no wickedness.'

Miriam knew vast tracts of the Bible; the Psalms, Song of Solomon, Ecclesiastes, Isaiah. The words had always stuck to her like burrs. 'So she caught him and kissed him and said unto him, I have peace offerings with me.'

It was a fine day but Miriam shivered in her despair. There was still no letter from Josi. Only one she'd had from him since his return to Hendre Ddu and that written in the first week. *Wait for me. Please wait for me. I love you.* She had worn out the scrap of paper by looking at it too often; she needed another letter, but he didn't write.

She knew what he must be suffering with his dying wife and his troubled conscience; she sympathized with him. But nagging at her was the thought that he should also be thinking of her in her loneliness and loss.

The acrid smell of autumn was in the air, a bonfire somewhere in the distance, chrysanthemums in cottage gardens. Leaves, though still on the trees, russet and gold, already smelled of the earth, the bracken and the few hedgerow flowers, campion and ragged robin, had the same wet, decaying smell. Seagulls circled above her, crying desolately; the sea was no longer a novelty, but a grey emptiness, a scar on the edge of the land.

Mrs Thomas had managed to get Miriam an old baby carriage from the house where she had been in service as a girl, and Miriam had spent hours pushing the baby along the quiet lanes, gathering blackberries and crab apples. But blackberries became devil's fruit in October and Mrs Thomas wouldn't have them. Hips and haws weren't worth the picking, though as a child she had eaten plenty of haws, 'bread and cheese and beer', on her hungry way from school.

'You have your baby,' Mrs Thomas would say whenever she saw

that Miriam was miserable. 'A lovely child. Perfect in every way.'

'She is. I know it.' Miriam would gaze at Mari-Elen for hours, as she waved her small fists about, or pursed her lips as though to begin a long dissertation. She was lovely. All the same, Miriam was disappointed in her – or in herself. The first day she had caught a glimpse of Josi on the tiny face; by this time there seemed no trace of him. Even her fingernails are like mine, she thought, her toenails, the shape of her ears. Loving her seemed only an extension of loving herself.

She wanted Josi. Loved him, only him. She had got used to his loving her. At first it had seemed a dream, his love, something too rare and glorious to be real. But she had got used to it, had learned to accept it; as Christians, though unworthy, accept the love of God.

If he had cooled towards her when he had first known about the baby, she might have got used to that, too, by this time. But he had never wavered, had insisted on taking her away, defying society. Oh, he had loved her.

The sun also ariseth and the sun goeth down.

'You have your baby,' Mrs Thomas always said, as though that made up for everything.

Miriam liked Mrs Thomas well enough, what she knew of her. She was a secret, solitary woman, though, disclosing little of herself in the seven or eight weeks they had lived together. She was poor, it was obvious that her sons had all but forgotten her; that's all Miriam knew. She made a little money by dressmaking.

In the evening, Miriam would do some hand-sewing for her while she was busy with the sewing machine which was her most treasured possession.

At first Miriam had been trusted only with the hemming, but had recently graduated to button-holes and fancy stitches; Mrs Thomas scrutinizing everything she did and occasionally rewarding her with a small, tight smile. She had mentioned paying for her help, but Miriam – receiving twenty-five shillings a week from Rachel Evans's solicitor – had refused to let her.

As well as helping with dressmaking, Miriam also did most of the housework. Partly because it passed the time, partly because she felt grateful to Mrs Thomas for giving her a home. She knew it wasn't easy for her; her neighbours talked, and she was dependent on the neighbours for work.

Mrs Thomas would volunteer no information about herself; neither about her childhood nor her married life, and wanted to hear nothing of Miriam's life. Miriam had once told her about her mother's poverty and early death, only to be cut short as though such personal details embarrassed her.

The previous week, though, they had been making a wedding dress together. The bride's mother had bought the material, a bright blue satin, six years earlier, after getting a particularly good price for the annual calf. 'The only time in my life for me to have any money I didn't already owe,' she'd told Mrs Thomas and Miriam. 'Twenty-three and sixpence it cost me, six yards at three and eleven, and Leyshon and the boys all needing boots, but they had to wait. Make it up pretty, won't you.'

The bride-to-be was a fat girl with a round, vacant face, but Miriam had taken the greatest trouble, whipping the neck and cuffs with a paler blue thread and smocking the yoke and shoulders.

'A wedding isn't everything,' Mrs Thomas had said, fearing that she was being carried away. 'It's not all roses.'

'Oh it is,' Miriam had said. 'A fine wedding is every girl's dream.'

'One they soon wake from, you believe me. Many girls get married and spend the rest of their lives wishing they hadn't. You think everyone is happy but you, but there's plenty of married women would leap at the chance to change places with you, I can tell you.'

It was the first time Mrs Thomas had spoken so freely to her.

'But what about the disgrace?'

'Disgrace? Oh, you're trying to trick me into saying there's no disgrace in doing what you've done. I won't do that. But I'll tell you this; there's plenty of disgrace inside marriage as well as outside it. I lived in Swansea for a few years while my husband was on the railway there, and I saw plenty of disgrace and heard it too, every Saturday night, especially among those priest-ridden Mary's children.'

'But among the Welsh, chapel-going people?' Miriam had persisted.

'You won't get me to say a word against the chapel; I know what you're after. But I'm not so narrow-minded not to realize that there's goodness and decency outside chapel as well as inside, outside marriage and inside it.'

It was the nearest they had got to intimacy; the only time when Miriam had felt that Mrs Thomas was on her side, and that her initial reluctance to have her as a lodger was that it might have an adverse effect on her livelihood, not that she herself had any real qualms about Miriam's character.

But the letter Mrs Thomas had received that morning had shown otherwise.

It was from her youngest son, Ifor. He had enlisted, he told her, and, finding himself stationed at Wrexham, intended coming home for a few days.

The letter seemed to have thrown Mrs Thomas into a state of near panic. She hadn't said much; had read the short letter to Miriam, that was all; but had spent the morning staring out of the window, then walking about clutching her side as though in pain. She had done no sewing, though the mourning dresses she had cut out the previous evening were urgently needed.

Mrs Thomas, Miriam felt sure, was agitated at the thought of her young son being under the same roof as a fallen woman. She felt she ought to leave, for a time at least. She felt she should return to Llanfryn to her Aunt Hetty, but couldn't face the questions and sermons she would have to endure. 'You'll be back, my girl,' the old woman had told her when she had left in June, 'Oh yes, you'll be back for sure. That man of yours won't stay away when he begins to feel the shoe pinching. He'll be back in his good farm before winter, you mark my words.' How could she return, to prove her right? How could she stay where she was, when her presence was so unwelcome?

In her anxiety, she had walked much further than usual and found herself, for the first time, in the neighbouring village; outside the little school.

Nostalgia overcame her as she drew up by the gate and heard the familiar sounds of children at work and at play; the older ones chanting a poem whilst the little ones clapped and sang to a tinkling piano. She seemed to smell the familiar smells; charcoal stove, chalk, dusty books, carbolic soap. She stood there listening and remembering until afternoon school ended with the Lord's Prayer and the clanging of desks and chairs. She rushed away then, conscious of what she had lost, She had enjoyed teaching, the children had liked her, she had liked them. And the schoolhouse,

146

only a small four-roomed cottage, was clean and cosy. She had been respected and independent. Now she was an outcast. For the first time, having nothing to uphold her, she felt it bitterly. Instead of retracing her steps, she walked on and on, weeping inside herself.

It was almost dark when she returned. ('Where have you been?' Mrs Thomas would say. 'You've kept that baby out too long. The days are drawing in.')

As she got near the cottage, Miriam could see a young man sitting on the low wall, looking out to sea. He was in khaki uniform, the first Miriam had seen. She thought it must be Mrs Thomas's son, home earlier than expected, but as she got nearer she realized it was Tom; Josi's son, Tom. Her heart started to pound. She hurried towards him. 'What is it?' she asked.

'I'm home for a week's leave,' he told her. 'Returning tomorrow.' She had no idea that he had joined the army. It seemed a strange thing to have done when his mother was so ill.

Uneasy, unable to make small talk, she waited for him to continue. But he didn't seem to have anything to tell her.

'I'm sorry I can't ask you in,' she said at last.

'That's all right. I have to get back anyway. I've got to get the seven o'clock train to Llanfryn. I'm going back to my regiment tomorrow.'

'I must feed the baby,' Miriam said. Elen had begun to whimper and shake her fists.

'I'd like to see her. May I?'

Miriam picked her out of the perambulator, turning her towards the sea and the setting sun. She blinked and stopped crying.

Tom examined her gravely. She was the first baby he had ever really looked at.

Why had he come? Miriam wondered. What news had he for her? He couldn't have come merely to see the baby.

'It's my mother,' he said at last. 'That's what I've come about; my mother. Even in the last few days I've been home there's been quite a change in her condition; she's sinking fast. She's in considerable pain most of the time.'

'I'm sorry,' Miriam said. 'I'm sorry.'

'I just wanted you to know how it is,' Tom said. 'So that you understand.'

'Thank you for coming.'

'So that you know how things are. How my father is.'

'I do understand. I really do.'

At any other time Mari-Elen would have appreciated being held up close to look at the blazing sky, but not now. She was hungry and cold and she began to cry hard and insistently. Her lower lip shook with indignation.

'I must go in. Thank you for coming. I do understand.'

Mrs Thomas said nothing when Miriam came in. Only took the baby while she took off her shawl and got ready to feed her. Afterwards she poked the fire and made her a cup of tea.

'I'm Mr Evans's son,' Tom had told her when he'd asked for Miriam. He had seemed quiet and well-spoken. It had made her wonder, and it was only a lifetime's reserve that prevented her asking Miriam what he had wanted with her.

Miriam felt Mrs Thomas's eyes on her and imagined her disapproval. Perhaps she would now think she was involved with two men. Luckily, she was beyond caring what anyone thought. How beautiful the setting sun had looked.... I just wanted you to understand.

Of course she understood. She didn't blame anyone.

The baby, still only five months old, sucked so vigorously that she seemed to be taking away her whole substance. She imagined herself being sucked away until only her skeleton remained. She could hear the sea outside.

The evening passed somehow. Another day almost finished. Almost finished. Like Josi's poor wife. And his son. Going to France, to kill or be killed. 'The minstrel boy to the war has gone.' She had taught that song to many classes of children, always moved by its pathos, never till tonight so moved.

She lay back in her chair, desire wounding her. Josi would never be the same with her again. She knew that. 'The way of an eagle in the air; the way of a serpent upon a rock, the way of a ship in the midst of the sea; and the way of a man with a maid.' The way of a man with a maid. Beautiful words. Like flowers. Like burrs.

Not that he would desert her. After a decent interval he would come for her, but it would be his duty to her and the baby which would bring him. The headlong love she wanted was dead. How could it be otherwise? What love was proof against righteousness and guilt? Lay not up for yourselves treasures upon earth, where moth and rust and guilt and righteousness doth corrupt. The urgent unquestioning love she wanted was dead. The wages of sin is death. They had disregarded everyone and everything in their passion, but the God of Israel neither slumbered nor slept.

She roused herself angrily. She wouldn't sink into that self indulgence; God keeping watch over her.

Life was without any plan, totally chaotic. God was the wheel in the sky, nothing more, in its drive she had been insignificantly torn aside like the skylark's nest by the harrow. I am poured out like water.

There was a sharp death taste in her mouth.

After Mrs Thomas had gone to bed, Miriam crept out of the house and walked towards the sea.

SEVENTEEN

Edward's marriage had an inauspicious beginning.

Rose was anything but a serene bride. A few hours before the wedding, she seemed to recover all her old spirit, feeling that her parents had taken advantage of her humiliating loss of nerve under arrest in order to get her safely off their hands, despising herself that she had allowed them to manipulate her into a marriage she wasn't ready for. She all but refused to go through with the ceremony, but once more she was not quite brave enough to act according to her conscience.

During their honeymoon in Devon, she confessed to Edward that she had married him largely out of weakness and fear, and was unable to accept his repeated assurances of sympathy or his insistence that marriage should not limit her opportunities in any way: she should continue to work for the Women's Movement in Oxford, where he, too, would throw himself into the struggle. He was unfailingly loving and undemanding, but couldn't help the occasional feeling that he had, perhaps, lost even more than she. Ten or eleven days passed bleakly by.

It was the imminence of war which brought them together.

Rose's cousin, Claire, had been studying in Europe for some months, and having missed their wedding, travelled to Devon to see them.

'We'll be at war in a few days,' she told them. 'The French are already mobilizing and we can't let them fight alone, the Germans are breaking treaty after treaty. When I was in Berlin it was already obvious that nothing was going to stop them. I'll never forget the mood of the crowd in the Unter den Linden, cheering and singing whenever a company of infantry or a squadron of horse went by. They're a people so full of aggressive energy that they're ready to surge through Europe. And it's up to us to stop them. England must unite with France to defend the freedom of the little nations.

To remain neutral would be treachery.'

Edward and Rose were fired by her patriotism. They read all the newspapers they had neglected and decided to cut short their honeymoon – they were to have spent a month in the West Country – in order to be back in London at the centre of things.

When they got off the train at Paddington, they realized that Claire's prediction had been proved right; the station was thronged with troops going to join their regiments, and the newspaper boys outside the station with their placards – 'War Official' – were being besieged by normally placid and sober citizens wrestling for copies of the evening paper. The King had already proclaimed that the Army Reserve should be called out on permanent service.

The next day, the Prime Minister, Mr Asquith, asked Parliament for power to increase the number of men in the army by half a million and Edward immediately decided to apply for a commission instead of returning to Oxford.

London seemed transformed. There was wholesale panic buying of food – even perishable goods – as though people expected an immediate invasion. German shops and businesses were boarded up, their owners gone. There were long queues of men standing for hours outside every recruiting office. Even the noises of London; the cries of street traffic, the hooting of horns, the screams of trains, seemed to have become more strident and aggressive.

Rose accompanied Edward as he went from one military garrison to another, waiting patiently and eagerly while he was interviewed, optimistic of the result even when he was despondent. At the end of the following week, when he succeeded in obtaining a commission in the Royal Artillery, she was immensely proud and happy. That afternoon, in the taxi-cab that took them back to her parents' home, she cried in his arms that she loved him.

A few days later, Rose managed to get work as a helper at the local hospital, and after passing a preliminary examination was accepted as a member of the Voluntary Aid Detachment.

She continued to live at home – the house her father had taken for her and Edward in Oxford had been re-let – and when he was free, Edward came from Woolwich to join her.

He looked older in his uniform, his hair was close-cropped and he had grown a thin moustache. They had much to talk about, the progress of the war engrossed them both; they were far happier

151

than they had been on their honeymoon.

Life was hectic for each of them. As a full-time VAD, Rose had to get up at six-thirty every morning to get to the hospital by eight, and did not return until seven or seven-thirty in the evening.

Though her body was often exhausted, she felt happy and liberated again. Only three months after suffering her traumatic breakdown, feeling her life empty and wasted, she had been given a second chance. She wasn't going to be a drawing-room wife after all, she was a person in her own right, involved, as Mr Asquith had said in Parliament, in the classless struggle to defend the civilisation of the world.

Her parents, naturally enough, were very anxious about her, resenting the fact that she seemed to be working as hard as any servant girl. However, she was now a married woman, so that their sense of responsibility was blunted. All in all, her father was rather proud of her, and even her mother talked about her at her tea parties, when the other women boasted about their soldier sons.

It was a warm, bright September that year. The British and French armies won victories on the Marne and the Aisne. *Allies advancing*, announced the newspaper headlines triumphantly. *Huge enemy losses*. Throughout the month, Edward was able to be with Rose several evenings a week and once or twice they managed to get a day off together. Rose hadn't begun to feel apprehensive on Edward's behalf; she was conscious only of the glory of his position as a leader of men.

At the beginning of October, Rose encountered wounded soldiers for the first time. They were classified as non-serious cases, and as she had no part in dressing their wounds, she soon got used to their weakness and pallor. It was the element of profound pessimism amongst them which disturbed and shocked her.

They called out to her and to the other nurses cheerfully enough, but left to themselves, they fell silent and morose, and when she had asked one of them about conditions at the Front, what it had been really like, he had flinched as though from a blow. 'It was hell,' he had said. 'Hell on earth. Don't ask about it.'

'Hell on earth.' The words echoed in her mind whatever she did that day. Her ideas of warfare had been so remote; men on horseback looking rather fine. Casualties of course, they were inevitable.

Pain and suffering, of course, nobly borne. But not fear. Stark, unhidden fear was something she hadn't considered.

That evening when she went off duty, Rose didn't run for the train with the other girls, but fell behind, letting them all go without her. She was feeling badly shaken and thought a solitary walk might help to steady her.

It was further to her home than she had thought. She had rarely been out on her own and was more nervous than she would have cared to admit.

Reaching familiar ground at last, she saw that there was a light on at the parish church and decided to go in.

The organ was playing and there were several people in the nave, listening to the music or praying. She sat at the back, not certain why she was there; she went to church on Sundays but didn't consider herself religious. Clergymen, being dyed-in-the-wool enemies of women's suffrage, had turned her against religion. It was churchmen, beginning with the insufferable Paul, 'therefore as the church is subject unto Christ so let the wives be to their own husbands in every thing', that she objected to, not the church. Certainly the atmosphere and the music were wonderful and there were words which stirred the soul. She tried to think of words to replace the 'Let *me* help. Let *me* work. Let *me*,' which were the ones always in her heart.

Looking up from her meditation, she noticed an officer sitting a few rows in front of her and as he turned his head, she saw that it was Edward. Filled with pleasure at the coincidence, she got up to join him. But before she had arrived at his side, he had got to his knees and was praying. She felt embarrassed, almost as though she were spying on him, and even considered moving away and leaving the church without disturbing him. He was praying so intently. She wondered if he was frightened like the soldiers at the hospital.

When he got up from his knees and saw her, he took her hand and smiled as though her being there was the most natural thing in the world. They sat for a while longer, listening to the organ music, thinking their own thoughts.

'You're not worried about anything?' Rose asked, as they walked the last quarter of a mile to her home. Edward was still strangely silent.

'Yes, a little. Everyone said we'd be in Germany by October.

153

Something seems to be going wrong.'

He didn't tell her of the accounts of trench warfare he had been given that morning by an officer newly returned from the Front: two sides facing each other, battering each other's defences in close combat, huge losses on both sides, continual conditions of checkmate, a rumour that Kitchener had said it could last three or four years.

'How could it?' he had asked. 'If there are such huge losses, both armies will be finished in no time. How could it go on?'

'By throwing in more and more replacements. There's no shortage of men. The government is already embarrassed by the number of recruits, it can't even equip them all. At the moment there are over a hundred thousand volunteers every month. All over the country they're still living under canvas and drilling in civilian clothes, walking sticks instead of rifles. There'll be no shortage of men, however many are killed.'

'It's not going to be as easy as we thought,' Edward said at last.

And Rose, the words of the wounded soldier she had questioned earlier, still in her mind, was unable to dispel his despondency.

'I'm going to join the Military Nursing Service,' was all she said. 'I must go to the Front.' As she spoke, her face was lit up by an overhead street lamp; to Edward, it seemed to glow with the fervour of her resolve. 'I'm so lucky to be able to help. I never, never thought to be so lucky.'

'We're both lucky,' Edward said, infected by her courage. 'We're the fortunate generation.'

They reached the house and ran up the front steps hand in hand.

When Edward, a week later, got Tom's letter telling him he was being posted abroad and asking him to meet him at Victoria that night, his instinct was to stay away.

He was immediately aware how much he longed for news of Catrin, how little, in spite of his wholehearted effort, he had succeeded in forgetting her.

He should keep away from the shadow of her influence: he knew it.

At the same time, he couldn't easily bring himself to disappoint Tom; dear old Tom, as always completely unaware of any possible complexities of any situation.

He was free and, of course, decided to go to Victoria. How could he have stayed away?

Tom was low in spirits. Though he knew Edward envied him his luck in going out to France, he could feel no joy or excitement at the prospect. He hoped not to disgrace himself, but expected no exhilaration or glory.

They sat in a pub near the station, departing soldiers all around them.

Edward asked after his family, but Tom could hardly bear to burden his friend with the sadness he had left behind him. 'Mother's no better,' was all he could bring himself to say. 'Father's losing himself in work. Miss Rees, well, she endures like a rock.'

'And Catrin?' Catrin's lovely face was suddenly so vividly before Edward that he held his breath.

'Oh, nursing in Cardiff as I told you. No, it wasn't really to do with the war. All she wanted was to be an art student, well, you know that. Then one morning she woke up with a serious vocation for nursing; it was as sudden as that. And Doctor Andrews begged me to let her go away because of Mother's illness. Perhaps it's better for her. I saw her this morning. Yes, she came to the railway station at Cardiff to see me off. She looked very tired, I thought. All the joy knocked out of her, I thought. Well of course, it's hard work, nursing. And she's young to be away from home.'

Edward had fallen silent.

'And Rose?' Tom asked, conscious of having talked only of his own family.

'Very well. Very happy. She's nursing too. She's applied to join the Military Service; she's determined to go out to France. She's given up her work for the Women's Movement; they all have. Mrs Pankhurst begged all her followers to switch their energies to the war effort. They're a hundred per cent behind the country now.'

Tom nodded his approval.

'I wonder if we'll meet in France?' he asked then.

'Of course we will. I'll get there somehow, don't you worry.'

Tom had to board the boat-train by eleven-thirty. Edward went on to the platform with him, standing there surrounded by mothers, wives and sweethearts. Morale was high.

Afterwards, Edward walked through the dark narrow streets near the station, feeling as miserably lonely as he had ever felt in his life.

When at last he hailed a passing taxi-cab, he returned to his barracks. 'Rose will be fast asleep,' he told himself. 'It would be irresponsible to wake her.'

EIGHTEEN

'I suppose you blame me,' Lily Thomas said.

Josi walked about the small, bright room as though he hadn't heard her. The last man on the earth he seemed, as he walked about the room, the whole universe dead around him.

Until then it was only Miriam she had pitied.

'Do you think I can spare you any part of the blame?' Josi said at last, his voice rough and tired.

'I'm not a friendly person, Mr Evans, I've dried up, that's the truth of it. But I wasn't unkind to her.'

'I never thought so.'

'I was unwilling to take her in at the beginning, I admit that. That was only natural, wasn't it. Anyone would have been the same, wouldn't they?'

He shrugged his shoulders.

'I liked her, Mr Evans. She was...'

There was a sudden flash of anger in his eyes; menace, as though he was forbidding her to touch Miriam with her charity.

Silence again.

'Do you want me to keep the baby here for a while?'

He seemed almost to have forgotten the baby. He looked at Mrs Thomas with a different expression; gratitude, a rare humility. 'I wasn't sure she'd still be here,' he said.

'Oh yes, I kept her here. She knows me, doesn't she. I knew she'd be all right with me. Would you like to see her? I could wake her and bring her down.'

'No, not tonight. Don't wake her tonight. I'll make arrangements for her very soon. I'll be in touch with you again very soon.'

Mrs Thomas could see him looking about for signs of Miriam,

'I'd like her things,' he said.

'I'll fetch them.'

She went upstairs and opened the drawer where Miriam kept her

157

clothes, all neatly folded. She carried them downstairs. 'Her box is in the shed,' she said, 'I'll go and fetch her box.'

She lit the hurricane lamp and went out.

While she was out, Josi picked up one garment after another, laying them to his face. They gave him nothing of her.

Mrs Thomas brought in the square green trunk, dusted it inside and out and laid the pile of clothes in it.

'I don't want them,' Josi said. 'No, I don't want them.'

'There's her books in the parlour.'

'I don't want them.'

'Oh, but you'll want them later, I'm sure. She was very fond of her books. I'll keep her clothes if you want me to. I'll wear them; I'll be glad to.'

She lifted the clothes out of the trunk again and put them on the table. Such a small pile they made. 'You have them,' Josi said. He knew that in offering to wear them, Mrs Thomas was showing the extent of her respect.

'Mr Davies the minister held a service here, Mr Evans. He couldn't have been kinder, not if she had been one of his members. "Judge not that ye be not judged." And a beautiful prayer.'

Josi shuddered to think how angry that would have made Miriam. But nothing can touch her now, he thought. He turned away from Mrs Thomas. He could hear the sea outside.

'Did anything out of the ordinary happen that day? Anything different? To make her do it, I mean?'

'I've asked myself that dozens of times, Mr Evans. Gone over it, minute by minute. It was an ordinary day. Well, no, not entirely. I had a letter from my youngest son that morning, telling me he had enlisted with the army. That upset me a lot because he's only eighteen and never been strong like the other two. The eldest one is thirteen years older and always been hard on him. I was afraid it was that that had made him join up. She knew I was worried, I suppose, though I didn't talk about it. Only just told her about the letter; read it to her, perhaps. I can't remember. Apart from that, nothing unusual happened.'

(She had decided not to mention Tom's visit in the evening. If his father wasn't already aware of it, it would give him something else to worry about; might cause more trouble in a family where

158

there was already too much.)

'She took the baby for a walk in the afternoon, came back, fed her and put her to bed. Then she had some tea and did some sewing for me. That's all. I left her downstairs reading. She would often stay down after me for ten minutes or so. I used to be cross with her about wasting the paraffin, but that night I didn't say anything; I was too worried about my son, I think. I just left her. "Good night", perhaps, nothing more. Next morning I woke and knew, I don't know how, that something was wrong. Even before the baby began to cry, I knew. And then I saw that her bed hadn't been slept in and I rushed out and found her shoes on the wall. And then I ran to get the old Captain from Ynys Hir to take his boat out and sent my neighbour's boy to Llys Howell for the police. I did everything I could, Mr Evans.'

'Yes. Everything you could.'

'That's all I can tell you. They found her on the Friday, as I told you. And the next day I opened the letter that came for her every week and wrote to the solicitor asking him to get in touch with you.'

'Yes. Thank you.'

She wanted to ask how long she would have the baby, whether she would be paid; money was short in the winter, not many people wanting new clothes, but didn't feel she could. She would write again to the solicitor in a week or two.

'I'm sorry to have troubled you,' Josi said then, in a flat, empty voice. 'I had to see you. I'll go now. Thank you.'

But when he got to the door, he changed his mind and came back. He stood near her for a moment with his hand on the table; then sat down heavily in the chair as though having no more strength even to stand.

A little nerve played in his cheek. Apart from that he was perfectly still.

'Did she talk to you about me?'

'No.'

'Nothing at all.'

Mrs Thomas, though she felt sorry for Josi, now only wanted to get rid of him. She knew he was trying to scratch comfort from somewhere, but she felt too drained of emotion to respond. She hadn't really responded to anyone since her husband had died sixteen years ago. She was willing to answer questions, to do her duty, but didn't feel she could do more; he had no right to expect it.

But he did expect it. He was still waiting.

'I know she loved you,' she said at last.

'How?' Josi winced, as though it was pain she had given him, not comfort. 'How can you know that? If she didn't talk about me.'

'A hungry person is the one to smell food, Mr Evans.'

'Is that all you can tell me?'

'That's all. She loved you, I know that.'

He sat with his head in his hands.

'You've got your little girl. Yours and hers. At the moment, I suppose you feel she's a bit of a problem; a big problem perhaps, but you'll thank God for her later on. She's going to look like her mother.'

Josi sat silent and still for several minutes so that Mrs Thomas wondered whether he could be physically ill. He still had his head in his hands. She wondered if he could be praying.

At last he got to his feet. 'I'll take her with me,' he said.

'Not tonight?'

'Yes, tonight. I've got a motor-car outside.'

'Who'll look after her?'

'I've got a good girl to look after her, don't worry about that. She'll be well cared for.'

'What about your wife?'

'It'll be all right.'

Mrs Thomas felt both regret and relief; she was fond of the little thing; all the same she had been worried about the time she would keep her from her sewing, worried about making ends meet.

She went upstairs again and brought down the baby and a bundle of little clothes.

'I've wrapped her up well. Are you sure it will be all right for you to take her tonight?'

'Yes, quite sure.'

She put the baby into his arms.

'She'll be well looked after,' Josi said again. Deriving a momentary sense of comfort from the warmth of the sleeping child, he looked up and thanked Mrs Thomas for her care.

She affected not to hear him.

'Here's her bottle. She drinks from it nicely now, though I had a lot of trouble last week.' She was finding difficulty in keeping her voice steady. She wanted them both out of her way.

The driver seemed surprised to see the baby in Josi's arms but said nothing, only hurried out to take the bundle of clothes from Mrs Thomas. 'It's a stormy old night, isn't it,' he said gravely. 'But I suppose you're used to it here. Yes indeed.'

Mrs Thomas and Josi shook hands and parted with no further word.

Mrs Thomas went back to her little cottage, made the fire safe, and went straight to bed. She lay awake for hours, though, pulling at the bedclothes, turning the pillows. I'm getting soft in my old age, she told herself angrily. What good will this ache in my blood and my bones do anyone?

Miss Rees and Lowri were still up waiting for Josi.

'Will you go down to see Sali's mother?' he asked Lowri. 'Eben's waiting outside to take you. Ask her whether she can come up to sit with Mrs Evans tonight. I want you to have the baby.'

'Sali's mother is here, Mr Evans,' Miss Rees said. 'Yes, I sent for her earlier on. She's upstairs with Mrs Evans now. Well, we were expecting the baby, weren't we? Where else should she be but here? And now give her to me, do. You're holding her too tightly. No wonder the little mite is crying. There, there, my little one, there, there. Lowri's got your milk and your bed all ready for you. There, there.'

Five days later Rachel Evans died. Tom had already let Catrin know how ill their mother was, so that being sent for, she came prepared for the worst.

'You can't want her to live any longer. You can't want her to live in this pain,' Miss Rees said over and over again to herself, and to everyone else, but all the time praying for a miracle. Catrin and Josi watched silently at the bedside, keeping their thoughts to themselves.

'*Mor hyfryd yw y rhai drwy ffydd. Sy'n mynd o blith y byw,*' Miss Rees recited. The old funeral hymn. 'How happy, they, in steadfast faith. Who leave the world's unrest. Their names are fragrant in the air. Their slumbers sweetly blessed.'

Rachel recognized no one in the last days, but those words she seemed to recognize. Once or twice they all felt that she seemed to be listening to them with an air of peace, almost of pleasure.

The funeral occupied and sustained Miss Rees over the next days. The great throng lining the road to the chapel, the four officiating ministers, the chapel crowded to the doors, the hymn-singing, faultless as singing at a festival, the profound silence at the graveside, the extravagant number of wreaths, the five women, all previous maids whom she had trained – and all in decent mourning – serving the traditional cold ham and beef in the house afterwards; all these things were balm to her sore heart. Josi's cast-iron silence and impassivity at the funeral, and his absence from the house afterwards, also seemed right. Although she felt sorry for him, she couldn't help feeling that his guilt was a measure of his redemption. (In her innermost heart – although she was ashamed of it, knowing it to be unChristian – a small, nasty voice insisted that Miss Lewis's suicide was also far from inappropriate.)

Catrin stayed home for a few days after the funeral, her mind numb with shock. To her the funeral had been almost unbearable; the mockery of grief. She was not yet nineteen and had always idolized her mother.

'How I wish you'd stay home with us now, Miss Catrin. How will we manage without you, and Mr Evans in such a way? What will we do? I'm sure I'm past everything and Lowri's got her hands full with the baby. Megan could manage her, she's a good little girl, but Mr Evans says Lowri, so there we are. And Sali's not up to the dairy work, you know that yourself, let alone the baking. I know Mr Evans will pull himself together soon, for Mr Tom's sake, but all the time he talks about leaving Hendre Ddu and going back to Cefn Hebog. What good will that do anyone? Lowri's mother won't let her go to that out of the way place you can be very sure, and when I tell him so, he says the baby will have to stay here with us and that he'll come over every day. Five or six miles to ride every day and winter upon us. It will break him, Miss Catrin; perhaps that's what he wants. But who'll look after the farm for Mr Tom if his own father doesn't? What a comfort it would be, Miss Catrin, if you could leave that old hospital and come home. And Doctor

Andrews would be so pleased too, and your father, you can be sure, and I can't help pitying him in spite of everything.'

'I simply can't, though, Nano. So many nurses are going to the military hospitals; we're getting terribly short-staffed. When the war is over, I'll come back, I promise you. And it can't last much longer. We could force the Germans back now, they say, but they think it's better to wait for spring, when they can get the New Army out there to finish the job properly. I'll be back in the spring or the summer, you shall see. I'll be back when she's a year old; Mari-Elen. She's lovely, isn't she, Nano? What terrible trouble she's caused and look at her smiling at everyone with her little gums. I was very cruel to her mother, Nano. I saw her in Llanfryn last summer and I was very cruel to her. I didn't have any right to speak to her as I did.'

'Well, I don't know about that, I'm sure. I know I'd have done the same anyway. Who could help it? I don't like to speak ill of the dead, but she has a lot to answer for. Who knows if your poor mother would have broken like she did if that woman hadn't taken your father away. I would have had a pretty sharp word with her if I'd have met her, I know that.'

'No, it was wrong of me. Unforgivable. It can't have been her fault. Father isn't a child.'

'The woman is always to blame. Always.'

'I can't see how you can say that, Nano. That seems very unfair.'

'It may be unfair. I think it is unfair. But it's the truth all the same. A man is always ready to take advantage, a woman must be strong and say no or there'll be no decency left. That's how it's always been and that's how it always will be. She wasn't a good woman, that's the long and the short of it. She shouldn't ever have come to Rhydfelen by rights. There's plenty of people will tell you that she taught next to no religion in her school and went to chapel only once in a blue moon. She only got the job because she had studied at home for a BA and what good is that for an elementary schoolmistress, I'd like to know. How much Latin did old Martin Williams know, but he was a wonderful schoolmaster; none of the children left him without the long multiplications and roods and chains and more things than I can name, and he was only put in the school because Sir Grismond ran over him one Christmas Eve and broke his good leg. It's character you want in a school, not booklearning. Martha Penbryn that used to wash for Miss Lewis told me that she used to read wicked books and novels. She wasn't wicked herself, I'm not saying so, or your father wouldn't have had anything to do with her, but she didn't have any stability to her. The balance of her mind was disturbed, as they said in the quest. But there you are, God is merciful, and the little one will be well cared for and loved too. Who could resist such a little doll, isn't it? Sidan bach Nano. Oh well, if only this old war was over and Mr Tom back home, I could make some sense out of it, somehow.'

NINETEEN

Tom's first letter to Edward from France contained news of his mother's death.

> Of course I expected to hear of it daily, but the sorrow is still as sharp. It was wrong of me to escape my responsibilities by coming out here where I can't feel really involved. I should be with my father. Poor Catrin, too. She writes bravely, but she's very young to be away from home at such a time. I know you'll write to her, Edward, try to comfort her. She looks on you as a brother. Everything has been quiet here for the past few days. I wish there wasn't so much time to brood.

Edward decided to go to Cardiff to see Catrin. He didn't try to convince himself that it was his duty, only that he had been given an excuse to do what he wanted and needed to do. Luckily he had a week-end leave prior to a posting to the South Coast.

He showed Rose the letter from Tom, telling her that he intended to see Catrin. Rose was worried about his undertaking the journey at a time when he should be resting. (He had recently undergone two weeks' field exercise with poor rations and very little sleep.) 'But I need to see her,' he told Rose, as though willing her, by the urgency in his voice, to question him. But she forbore, or saw no reason to do so. 'I'm so glad that she's training to be a nurse,' was all she said. 'If she were at home, leading an idle and useless life, think how much worse it would be for her.'

The first available train on the Saturday morning was crowded with soldiers and civilians; the war had already brought about fewer trains and more passengers, and everyone seemed tense and over-wrought. The November day was cold and foggy.

Edward decided to tell Catrin the truth about what had happened after he left Hendre Ddu the previous June. He realized

165

that he had been foolish, even cruel to pretend that what had been between them was nothing but a holiday flirtation which had died its natural death. Because admitting or even thinking about the truth had been too painful, he had debased something fine and beautiful.

If he had done wrong in marrying Rose, and he supposed he had, he had done it because it had seemed necessary: Rose's spirit had been broken and his instinct, as well as his duty, had been to protect and console her. He would tell Catrin that. To speak the simple, unvarnished truth could surely not be wrong or dishonourable. He couldn't face the thought of going out to France before it was done.

He stood in the corridor, a bitter excitement struggling with the sadness and confusion in his mind. He thought about the war. He'd believed, like most other people, that it would be over in a matter of months. It had seemed a privilege, an honour, to fight for one's country. By this time, it seemed only a grim necessity. Perhaps it was better to be stripped of false illusion. Even Rose, now that she was actually nursing the wounded, seemed more often outraged than excited by the war.

How complicated life was, how ambivalent every motive, every action. He thought about Rose, whom he admired, loved, though not ardently, and who, hating men, loved him in her own way. When he had decided to marry her instead of breaking off their engagement, the shock of disappointment he had felt at losing Catrin was not unmixed with relief that he was, after all, embarked on the easy, safe, approved, conventional way. He thought about Tom, his blunt, unimaginative friend who was in France ready to kill or be killed because he hadn't been able to watch his mother's suffering. About Catrin, with her longing for pleasure and success, who had suddenly dedicated herself to a difficult and badly-paid profession; sickened perhaps by the ease with which he had seemed to slip in and out of love, soured perhaps in her high expectation of life. Tom, who noticed little, had said she seemed to have lost all her joy. Oh, and if she was unhappy on his account, how could he bear not to comfort her? Was he strong enough to behave properly towards her? Perhaps it would be better, even now, if he stayed away from her. But he couldn't stay away from her.

Suddenly, in the middle of his troubled thoughts, fighting against a need to sleep, one clear fact emerged like a light: he was on his way to see her. He was travelling towards her. He would look on her beauty again and talk to her and hear her lovely voice. He was so filled with joy and warmth that, opening his eyes, he was amazed to find the day still grey and foggy, the people around him still downcast and self-absorbed. Even if I only speak to her about her mother's death, she will know why I came, and if I never see her again, I shall always be glad that she knew.

His exalted mood lasted for the remainder of the long, uncomfortable journey.

When he arrived at the hospital, he asked for the matron and was taken to her office. He explained his wish to see Nurse Evans, producing the letter he had received from her brother. The matron, who already had a soft spot for the poor motherless girl, was pleased that her brother's friend, and quite the gentleman, had taken the trouble to visit her. Instead of sending him to the probationers' common room where officially approved visitors could be entertained, she showed him into her private sitting-room – flowers on the table, a good fire in the grate – and had someone fetch Catrin there.

'I'll send you some tea, Lieutenant. Nurse Evans may stay with you for half an hour. It was good of you to travel from London to see her.'

She returned to her office.

Catrin knocked at the door of the matron's sitting-room and went in. Told that there was a young officer waiting to see her, she had thought it would be Tom, home on leave because of their mother's death. When she saw Edward in the room, she stopped abruptly, raising her hands to her throat.

'Dear Catrin,' Edward said. 'Is it such a terrible shock?'

He led her to a fireside chair and sat down opposite her. He felt light-headed with pain and joy; it was only the entrance of a maid bringing a tray of tea that kept him from breaking down completely, from crying at her feet that he loved her.

The maid poured out the tea and left them.

'I had to see you,' Edward said. 'Please say something. Say something, Catrin. Please.'

For an instant, he had been disappointed at her appearance; she seemed less radiant than his mental image of her. Her face was paler than ever, she looked older and thinner. Within seconds, though, he knew that her essential beauty was unimpaired, was, perhaps, even more formidable; her cheek bones finer, her lovely green eyes more expressive, more tenderly luminous, in her dear, wan face.

'I heard about your mother's death. I was so sorry. Tom asked me to write to you but I decided to try to see you instead.'

Catrin nodded her head gravely, and when at last she spoke, her clear, young voice gripped his heart as much as her appearance.

'Tom shouldn't have troubled you. You must be very busy, very tired. You look tired.'

'I had to see you again, that's the truth of the matter, I mustn't pretend otherwise. Oh, don't be angry. I had to see you again. I felt I had to tell you what happened when I left Hendre Ddu last June.'

'You needn't tell me. Please. You mustn't feel you owe me an explanation. I can understand how it must have been for you.'

'Rose was under arrest and frightened.'

Edward told his story very simply. As he spoke, his eyes never left hers.

'So, you see, it was impossible to do what I intended. I had truly intended to tell Rose, and my parents and hers, about you. But it was impossible to do anything except what I did.

They sat staring at each other.

'Do you understand, Catrin, what I'm trying to say? Catrin, you must tell me that you understand. I had to see you to tell you that I meant every word I said when I left you at Llanfair, though I can never say those words again. Will you believe me, Catrin?'

'I'll try. Oh, I'd like to try.' Catrin's voice was hardly audible.

'Tell me you believe me, Catrin. Tell me you believe what I can't say. Please tell me you believe me and it will always comfort me. Wherever I go, whatever happens, I'll remember that you understood.'

'Yes, I believe you, Edward. I do understand. Thank you for coming to tell me. I'm glad you did. I'll always be glad you did.'

'Now I must go, I suppose. I've seen you again, heard your voice. My dear girl. Remember what was between us for one half-hour. That can never pass away. I must go. Oh, I must go now.'

Edward got to his feet. He held out his hand, but withdrew it without touching hers.

'You can't leave me,' Catrin said, her voice trembling.

He turned and took her into his arms and for what remained of the short half-hour, they clung together.

TWENTY

After their brief meeting in November, Catrin and Edward started writing to each other; their letters, though, containing no references to their bewildering love.

Catrin wrote about her work in the wards, her desire to excel in the first year examinations, about her colleagues and patients, about her occasional week-ends at home, her delight in her little half-sister. She wrote every night, however tired she was; the letters she actually sent him being only short, carefully chosen extracts from her long outpourings. Through that hard, lonely winter after her mother's death, writing to Edward seemed the most real part of her life.

Edward, in his letters, reminisced about his life at Oxford with Tom, and about his summer days at Hendre Ddu, every moment of which seemed engraved on his memory. From time to time he included a fleeting mention of the war; of the first German air raid which had occurred just before Christmas and which had plunged London into darkness; once or twice a hint that France loomed ahead of him.

Edward was sent to the front line within a week or two of his arrival in France in March 1915.

After a few weeks of living in a trench, the monotonous food, the scarcity of water, the lack of privacy, the almost continual noise of rifle and shells, no one talked or thought of patriotism or glory. Such abstract ideas seemed absurd, part of another existence, real life shrank to a fight for survival, silent endurance became every man's aim.

Edward didn't mention, in his letters to Catrin, the terrible sights he was witnessing almost daily; dead colleagues who were almost unrecognizable, wounded men even more pitiable because still alive.

He wrote to her about the larks they could hear singing, still

170

singing, over the dull roar of the heavy guns, about the clusters of bluebells that could be found here and there even on the walls of the trenches, about the books he was reading, paragraph by paragraph, the poetry he was trying to write. He told her his closest thoughts, 'Life can't be so frail that it can be quenched by a stray bullet or a piece of shrapnel. Surely it can't. There must be something more. It has taken a war to make me recognize the eternal in life, the river that flows through us all, so that there is no real end.'

She knew his letters by heart. They were like a cloak around her. She had no idea whether she would ever see him again, she had no premonition either of his death or his safety; it seemed enough that she was able to write to him and receive his letters. Sometimes there would be an interval of several weeks between them, but then she would receive two or three together and she would keep them unopened all day in the inside pocket of her apron, waiting for the time when she could be alone to read them. On those days nothing was too much trouble for her.

She also heard from Tom. Tom seemed to be pre-occupied with the past and the future, hardly mentioning the present.

Do you remember how we got up at four o'clock in the morning to have a last look at the kite's nest before I went back to school? What year was that? How old were we then? I have a vivid picture of you racing along trying to keep up with me, your hair unplaited and blowing all about your face. Father used to say it was like the mane of a mountain pony, do you remember? Do you remember the day I caught a fourteen-pound salmon in Pwll-y-Graig? What a day that was. When you next go home, will you ride over to Garth to see how the saplings are doing? Tell Glyn to clear the undergrowth if they seem choked. How strange that no one of our family is left in Hendre Ddu now, unless we count the baby. We must count the baby, I suppose. On the whole, I'm quite glad to think of her there with Nano and Lowri. I hope to meet your pretty friend Gwenllian when I come home, I'm sorry she doesn't feel she can write to me, but I appreciate her sentiments. The war creates enough difficulties without adding to them by forcing relationships which should be slowly and carefully nurtured. I intend to see her, though, when I come home.

You see, I intend to come home. And when I do, I shall be like old Prosser, never venturing beyond Erw Fach Bridge. I think a man is essentially the product of the area that begets him. I seem to have forgotten Shrewsbury and Oxford. It's men like old Abiah Prosser and Father I think about, women like Nano. And Mother, too, of course. I had hardly thought of myself as Welsh before – except at the International Rugby matches – had never thought of myself as different from my friends at school, and university. Now, I think of myself as the product of a different society, not better, not worse, but completely different, with a completely different history. Our grandparents, all four of them, spoke only Welsh, had never been out of Wales. How well worth preserving these differences seem to be. When I think of the civilization we're fighting for, I can only think about the patch I know best. I like to think of its radical tradition, its passion for learning; all the craftsmen and labourers who tried to make an academy out of the village chapel. I'm sure the sterner religious element was negative and cramping in many ways, that's why I stress that the society was different, not necessarily better, all the same, something about it was fine and worth preserving. And yet I am here with Welsh chaps whose families in one or two generations in industrial South Wales have completely lost their language and presumably with their language their consciousness of being different, their own special way of life. It seemed so strange that in this place, with all hell's forces of destruction let loose about me, I should be concerned with things like the language and culture of our unimportant small country: I suppose we must all fix on something to keep us sane.

Do you remember that Russian play we went to see on our last holiday together? Chekov, wasn't it? All the characters in it were longing for Moscow, just as you afterwards longed for London, London, London. I suppose it's some state of grace we really want, some Nirvana. I know I long for Carmarthenshire, for Hendre Ddu. All I want is to stand and watch the green film on the ploughed acres which a few weeks before seemed as hard and dead as cement. And then the ripening wheat. My Nirvana, I suppose.

In May, Catrin tried and passed her first year examinations. Through the early summer she remained fairly optimistic, happy that time was passing. She was sure the war couldn't last much longer. Life went on, mornings creeping into afternoons, afternoons sinking into night.

In August she had a fortnight's holiday in Hendre Ddu, and when

Doctor Andrews proposed to her again she promised to marry him in two years' time, after she had completed her training. She felt she would make a good doctor's wife. Besides, she liked him. Besides, no girl wanted to be alone all her life. She received his diamond ring, and before the end of the holiday went with Miss Rees to have tea at his house. He seemed a reassuring presence. As for Doctor Andrews, he was delighted that she seemed far less emotional, far more mature, than during the previous summer. She has, after all, a great deal of her mother about her, he thought. He was by this time convinced of her suitability as a wife. He was also in love with her.

He knew nothing of the letter she had received at the beginning of July, just after Edward's death in action. Edward's wife, Rose, had forwarded the unposted letter to her after receiving it among her husband's personal effects.

> My dear girl,
>   I have found an inch of candle and a quiet corner so that I can write to you again. As always, you are in my mind.
>   There is to be an offensive tomorrow. Somehow, I don't feel frightened once it has begun. Beforehand, though, I feel the need of wine and music – Captain Fielding has a gramophone and some Bach records – and more than either, and more than sleep, and more than prayer, I need this communication with you. The greatest blessing in my life is to have loved you. This morning early I wrote to Rose. She will understand, I know. All the confusion falls away. My candle is flickering, but I don't need a light. You fill the emptiness around me.

'*My dear Catrin*,' Rose had written in a covering letter, '*Edward was killed in action on the 22nd of June. He was my dear and loving friend. We must both try to be brave.*'

Her room mate had told the sister of their ward that Catrin had received bad news about a friend at the Front, and she was excused duties and allowed to stay in her room. For two whole days she did nothing but look at Edward's letter and hold it to her cheek. On the third day, she bathed her eyes, burned the letter and returned to her duties. In old age she would still remember Edward, golden and

173

perfect, as the love of her life. She knew that. The letter, like all his letters, was a part of her.

'Yes, he's a good, honourable man,' Nano told Catrin when they came home from visiting Doctor Andrews. 'Your poor mother would be very pleased about your engagement to him, I know that. He was as kind as an angel to your poor mother. Mr Tom's friend, now, Mr Turncliffe, yes, he was a flower among men, he was indeed, but Doctor Andrews is respected and kind and he leads a lonely life, you can tell that, and your poor mother thought the world of him. No, no, there's no need to cry. A good, hard-working doctor and a lovely house too.'

TWENTY-ONE

All through the winter Josi stayed in Cefn Hebog alone. Miss Rees sent young Dan up every week with a sack of food for him, but each time the boy had to leave it outside the locked door of the little farm house. For over four months Josi saw no one.

Days and nights passed by, leaving no mark. He walked and worked, usually in snow, during the short days, collecting sticks and chopping wood, and sat at a fire during the long nights without even a dog for company. For weeks he didn't sleep except in snatches at the fireside. His sweat dried on his body. He worked and sweated again. He never washed.

He had no bed; no furniture except for a few broken odds and ends the previous tenants had left behind. After his wife's funeral, his need to escape had been so urgent that he had taken nothing with him but a couple of blankets. Miss Rees sent him clean clothing from time to time, and soap and candles, but except for bare essentials he left everything untouched. He ate bread and cheese, made porridge, until his saucepan burned through, drank spring water.

He derived a certain satisfaction from the idea of being an outcast; he needed to feel that he was being punished, ostracized from society. If he thought at all, he imagined that he would spend the rest of his life there, alone. But he tried not to think. Collecting enough firewood on that isolated snow-bound moorland was an arduous task that filled his mind. The snow and the wind filled his mind.

Then, in the second week of March, some spring force, an insistent bird or some green growth, jolted him out of the death-wish of his existence and he began to think again of Hendre-Ddu which he had left to Jâms and Davy Prosser, and of his family. He washed himself and shaved, burned his old clothes and found new, swept out of his kitchen the accumulated debris of months, and decided to return to the work he knew and the familiar faces. In the space of a morning he had realized that his self-imposed exile was nothing but an indulgence; that he had to live, thinking and working, through his guilt and grief.

When he returned to Hendre Ddu that afternoon, ready to take over the management of the farm, though still determined never to live there again, he found Mari-Elen at ten months old already a little girl, tottering about and looking up at him with Miriam's clear, unshifting gaze. She had gone to him at once as though aware of the relationship between them, and had clung to him when he had got ready to leave that evening. After that, the one necessity of his life was to find a way to have her with him.

Even on that first day, he realized that he would have to marry Lowri. She was the one he had – almost sub-consciously – chosen to look after his daughter: it followed that she must be his choice as a wife. A little girl needed a woman to care for her and a poor man couldn't afford a housekeeper or even a nursemaid. It had to be Lowri, if she'd have him.

Cefn Hebog had to be renovated; the roof repaired, window panes replaced, papered inside and white-washed out, before anyone could decently live there, and Josi set himself to the task. He worked at Hendre Ddu every morning – he had slipped back with the greatest ease to his old routine – then spent his afternoons at his own small-holding.

In May, when the weather was warm, he had Lowri bring Mari-Elen up there on the pony so that while he worked he could watch her staggering about the yard or sleeping on the grass in the little walled garden.

He cleaned out the pond and brought up some ducks and ducklings. After putting the cow shed in order he went to Llanfryn mart and bought two cows and a white heifer.

Mari-Elen seemed to love being with him, mistress of all. The open moorland was beautiful in late spring and summer; larks sang without ceasing and the tiny streams were clear and cold.

He tried not to think how idyllic it could have been. Perhaps it could never have been idyllic. Perhaps Rachel's illness and death had affected him more deeply than anyone, except Miriam, had understood. He tried to live in the present, tried not to think of how it might have been.

It was late September when he asked Lowri to marry him; the cottage was ready, the garden dug and planted. 'Let me know your answer tomorrow,' he said. 'You can go home to talk it over with your parents tonight.'

He wished he could make his proposal sound less like a business transaction, but he realized that to kiss her or touch her in any way would be to overwhelm her entirely. Many times he had tried to hint at what was in his mind, but it had obviously been useless; she could not have been more surprised if he had told her that he intended marrying Miss Rees.

'How old are you?' he had asked her.

'Twenty-two.'

'Perhaps there's someone else you'd rather marry? You can tell me, you know. I won't be offended. Jâms perhaps?'

'No. Oh, no.'

'You're very fond of Mari-Elen and she thinks the world of you. Being married won't be too bad. You don't hate me, I know that.'

But Lowri looked so miserably embarrassed that he was tempted to let her off the hook, to tell her he could easily find someone else, someone a bit older, perhaps.

'Think about it, anyway,' he said at last. 'Let me know tomorrow. I'm much too old for you, I know, and I may have done some things that you and your parents don't much like, but on the other hand....'

He got stuck. He didn't care to bring seventeen acres of hard land and a small stone cottage into the reckoning, and he couldn't bring himself to lie about the state of his heart.

'But on the other hand, it would suit me very well,' he continued abruptly. And he nodded to her and smiled, and hurried from the room. He knew she would accept him.

And sure enough, she stood before him next morning blushed, and said, 'My parents and I thank you and we would like to accept your offer.'

It was what he had expected and wished for, but his heart lurched and his throat burned.

Before he could say anything, though, Mari-Elen found them – Lowri never managed to escape from her for long. She ran to them; she still hadn't quite mastered the trick of walking, she ran to them, and fell at their feet.

'Will you come to live with me in Cefn Hebog, sweetheart?' Josi asked her, swinging her up into his arms. She smiled, jigging herself up and down to show her eagerness, then collapsed on his chest, her lips on his face.

'She's a lot more enthusiastic than you are,' he told Lowri. 'Now, while there's no one in the kitchen, I think I'll have a kiss from you as well.'

'Oh, no.'

He pulled her towards him but she was too shy to kiss him. All the same, she laughed and coloured and the distance between them was bridged.

For days Lowri was afraid to tell Miss Rees her news, afraid of her anger or scorn. Finally, Josi told her, and to Lowri's surprise she seemed to have expected it and to think it a good idea.

She did not, however, waste any time on congratulations.

'Now, Lowri,' she said as soon as Josi had left the kitchen. 'The thing I always want you to put first is your duty to Mari-Elen. We won't talk about her mother; we never have done, and I'm not going to start now, but I know you'll understand me when I say you must bring the child up with even more than the usual care, to go to chapel and Sunday school and to learn her verses and to love God above everything. Mr Evans is a good religious man at heart, and if you are strong in your faith he will follow your example. Remember that Mari-Elen is half-sister to Mr Tom and Miss Catrin and you must bring her up accordingly. Caring for the animals on the clos and the dairy work and the cleaning are what most farmers' wives put first, their children fending for themselves quite early, but you mustn't ever let Mari-Elen go about in rough old clothes and dirty boots, or let her hang about for her meals. Remember that I'm here to help you and I will always have a bit put by for her because she is Mr Tom's half-sister, so it's only right and proper she should have everything she needs. You will be a good housewife, I know, because you've been trained to do things right. Many times you've said to yourself, that old Miss Rees, but you'll live to thank her, indeed you will. Some girls think that getting married is dressing up in fancy clothes and stopping for a cup of tea at three o'clock; it's those who get miserable when they wake up to the reality. You have more sense than that. Remember the proverb which is at the back of every tidy wife: a change is as good as a rest. When you've been carting out after the cows, now, or scrubbing the dairy, then it's a rest to do some baking or some ironing, but if you're foolish enough to sit idle with your hands in your lap, you won't catch up with yourself all week. But you'll be all right, I'm sure of it. Even your bread is much better than most girls', and though we all know that a man cannot live on bread alone, no man can live on shop bread even if it's brought round to your door twice a week, which it won't be up there in Cefn Hebog. Another thing, Lowri, while I remember....'

At the wedding service in Lowri's chapel, the squat little brown chapel he had gone to as a boy, Josi hadn't been able to keep his mind off Miriam. She had scorned Christian wedlock, and to him, too, the words seemed empty and faintly ridiculous. He looked at Lowri at his side, a stranger in a new light-coloured dress and blue Sunday hat. When the minister elicited her promise to love, honour and obey, Josi wanted to apologise to her. Who was he that she should obey him, let alone honour, let alone love.

'That was a lot of old nonsense, wasn't it,' he whispered to her as soon as he could, squeezing her arm. But her eyes were full of tears. Dear God, he thought with terror, she's in love with me, is it possible? I'm old enough to be her father and I've hardly considered her at all.

For the rest of the day, while they were at her mother's, he stayed near her, glancing at her from time to time as though he were an ordinary bridegroom, trying to eat what was put in front of him, smiling when that seemed necessary.

Lowri's sisters had all come home for the wedding, there were four girls between Lowri and Megan, the youngest. Lowri's mother had been in school with Josi. Once plump and pretty, she was now thin and faded with darting, uneasy eyes. She kept on saying how much she was looking forward to a grandson after all the girls she'd had. Her husband was considered one of the most intelligent men in the area; he had been destined for the ministry, but had had to leave college to get married. He was the foreman in the woollen mill at Henblas. They were a respected, hard-working couple.

Josi wondered why they had let Lowri marry him; it seemed a

179

careless way to dispose of a first-born whom they should have guarded and cherished.

Miss Rees was the guest of honour, and apart from Josi himself and possibly Lowri seemed the only one less than happy. She was probably thinking of the other wedding almost twenty-five years before, the grand reception at the Grosvenor Hotel afterwards, the other bride. He and Miss Rees were pre-occupied with ghosts. Poor Lowri's troubles were at least of flesh and blood. I'm frightened as well as you, he wanted to tell her. Of minutes that are black with pain, nights that seem endless, regrets that squeeze at the heart. Miriam.

He took Lowri's hand and patted it. He touched the ring on her finger.

'You two can go now,' Lowri's mother said. Josi wondered if she was jealous of her daughter, she seemed so intent to embarrass her. Plenty of women had wanted him, perhaps she had. He looked at her coldly.

'Is Sali keeping Mari-Elen tonight?' she asked.

'Of course not. She's coming with us. She doesn't like Sali.' Josi tightened his grip on Lowri's hand. She was a good girl.

'A night or two wouldn't make any difference.'

'Yes, they would. She's only one and a half.'

Josi left Lowri and her mother together. 'What are you thinking about, Miss Rees?' he asked the old woman. He found a chair by her side.

'I'm thinking how fond I am of you.' she said.

'You're not jealous of me any more. That's what it is.'

'I suppose you're right. You see, I never thought you were good enough for her. Now that I see you in your own light, I like you.'

'Well, I'm Mr Tom's father anyway, so I've had my uses.'

Her laugh rang out. It was a long time since he had heard it and it cheered him.

Lowri's grandfather sat by the fire, squat and black and unsmiling. His daughter-in-law had put him in his chapel coat that morning and polished his face with a piece of flannel. He was still angry. He spat into the fire from time to time. Josi took over the tin of tobacco he'd brought for him. At Lowri's request.

'Are you going to the war?' the old man asked, puzzled by the gift.

'Too old, man,' Josi said.

'Too old?' The old man cleared his throat noisily.

'You think I should fight, do you?' Josi asked, amiably.

'For the bloody English. No.' The little man spat squarely into the flames. 'They wanted me to fight once; against the Russians, I think, or the Turks. Not I. My family fight against the bloody English, not for them. My father burnt his ricks in the tithe war, ready to starve rather than pay the tithes.'

'It was the church you were fighting then.'

'Same thing, church and state. My grandfather was one of 'Becca's maidens in the hungry forties. They were fighters if you like. Pulled down all the bloody toll gates. Dressed as ladies, but it couldn't hide their men's hearts. Toll gates. Bloody English.'

'Lloyd-George is a good little man to my way of thinking,' Josi said peaceably, 'and he's one of the English now.'

'Turn-coat from the North.'

'Good little man to my way of thinking,' Josi said again. 'Not my business, though. Not today.'

The old man spun round to face him, the light of understanding in his eyes at last.

'You're the bridegroom, are you?'

'Aye,' Josi said. 'That's right.'

'You old ram.'

'Will we tell her about Miriam later on?' Lowri had asked Josi as they'd tucked Mari-Elen up in her new bedroom that night. She was the only one who had ever mentioned Miriam in his presence.

And hearing her name spoken, after so long a silence, had a strange effect on him. 'No,' he'd said, 'I don't think it will be necessary. It would only confuse her.'

He had felt the pain engulfing him again, but when it had eased a little he had taken Lowri to the other bedroom and closed the door, and the encounter he had only been able to think about with dread was accomplished with some love, some passion.

She was a sweet, simple girl, still calling him Mr Evans most of the time. She was distantly related to him, her mother was his second cousin, she had the same pretty colouring as the women in his family.

He would be good to her, see that she never had to work too

hard. He would have no qualms about taking whatever he wanted from Hendre Ddu. He still regarded himself as the boss there; he'd take his wages in kind. He certainly didn't intend to kill himself or have Lowri slave away to make Cefn Hebog self-sufficient.

Tom had written to say that if he was killed in the war, Hendre Ddu would be his. But he didn't intend to take it, come what may. If the worst happened, he would let Catrin have it. She and Andrews could live there and let Jâms Llethre and Davy Prosser manage the farm between them. He was sorry that Catrin intended marrying Doctor Andrews, though he had nothing tangible against him. Perhaps she loved him, though he thought it more likely that she didn't. Some people could do without love, he supposed. Perhaps he could have done without it if Miriam hadn't come into his life with her acorn-coloured eyes and skin, and her spirit like steel. 'Like the white blossom on the black thorn,' he sang softly, longing for her.

Lowri was unused to sleeping alone. At Hendre Ddu she had slept with Sali and Megan; with Mari-Elen in her cot on the far side of the room; at home she had always slept with at least three of her five sisters. She wished Mari-Elen would wake and cry so that she could fetch her; she was as soft and warm as a puppy. She mustn't fetch her, though, in case Josi came back to bed.

'Your breasts are lovely,' he had said earlier, 'lovely. You mustn't be shy with me, Lowri. I expect you'll have a baby yourself quite soon. You'd like that, wouldn't you?'

'Yes,' she had said. 'I'd like that. Yes.'

But what she really longed for was the night he would turn to her and sleep by her side instead of going up to the loft where he had slept as a boy and walking about there until she had fallen asleep. But she knew she mustn't expect it all at once. She had often seen Miriam Lewis, Rhydfelen, and had thought her beautiful. Not in the same way as Miss Catrin, who turned her beauty on you like a lamp, but in a secret way you could almost miss, a way you could hardly describe; the silence after a blackbird's song, a blue coil of smoke in the woods, the faint scent of flowers in the night. She didn't suppose a man could forget a woman like that in a hurry; she would be in his bones.

So she sighed as she looked at the dipping moon through the

small, uncurtained window. Nothing is ever perfect, she said to herself. Nothing is ever quite perfect. Miss Catrin was going to marry Doctor Andrews, she said, but her eyes were empty and hard. I'm the lucky one it seems to me, she told herself. It's as though I've been chosen, somehow.

The white light of the moon ennobled her plain, good-natured face. She put her hand across the empty space at her side and smiled and fell asleep.